"Why?" he asked, speeding up. In fact, she sped up, so she was almost running. He increased his own pace, then caught her arm.

"Is it some great secret?" Luca demanded. "You don't want me to meet your child?"

She stared at him with such wide eyes and such *fear* that his instinct kicked into overdrive again. There was something going on here. Something he had to understand.

With a last glance at her pinched pale face, he moved around the stroller so he could see the child for himself.

He almost passed out. Sitting there, beaming out at the world with dark, dark eyes and soft brown ringlets, was a toddler who was the spitting image of his little baby sister, Angelica, a child he hadn't seen in twenty-one long years.

And he knew.

He knew in that way one simply knows the incontrovertible facts of life that the little girl sitting in the stroller smiling up at him was his daughter.

He had a child.

He was a father.

Clare Connelly was raised in small-town Australia among a family of avid readers. She spent much of her childhood up a tree, Harlequin book in hand. Clare is married to her own real-life hero, and they live in a bungalow near the sea with their two children. She is frequently found staring into space—a surefire sign she is in the world of her characters. She has a penchant for French food and ice-cold champagne, and Harlequin novels continue to be her favorite-ever books. Writing for Harlequin Presents is a long-held dream. Clare can be contacted via clareconnelly.com or on her Facebook page.

Books by Clare Connelly

Harlequin Presents

Emergency Marriage to the Greek
Pregnant Princess in Manhattan
The Boss's Forbidden Assistant
Twelve Nights in the Prince's Bed
Pregnant Before the Proposal
Unwanted Royal Wife

The Long-Lost Cortéz Brothers

The Secret She Must Tell the Spaniard
Desert King's Forbidden Temptation

Brooding Billionaire Brothers

The Sicilian's Deal for "I Do"
Contracted and Claimed by the Boss

The Diamond Club

His Runaway Royal

Visit the Author Profile page
at Harlequin.com for more titles.

BILLION-DOLLAR SECRET BETWEEN THEM

CLARE CONNELLY

Harlequin

PRESENTS

Harlequin®
PRESENTS™

Recycling programs for this product may not exist in your area.

ISBN-13: 978-1-335-93973-9

Billion-Dollar Secret Between Them

Copyright © 2025 by Clare Connelly

Harlequin Enterprises ULC
22 Adelaide St. West, 41st Floor
Toronto, Ontario M5H 4E3, Canada
www.Harlequin.com

Printed in Lithuania

MIX
Paper | Supporting responsible forestry
FSC® C021394

BILLION-DOLLAR SECRET BETWEEN THEM

CHAPTER ONE

EVEN WITHOUT TURNING AROUND, Luca Romano knew what he'd see. He would recognise her voice anywhere—despite not having heard it for almost exactly three years. There was something in her tone—husky, sultry without trying to be, honest and emotional—that evoked an instant, visceral reaction.

Just like the first night they met.

He clutched the Scotch and, in an exercise in restraint, continued to stare straight ahead, his eyes focused on the bottles of liquor that lined the back wall of the bar. All the while, Imogen crooned a slow ballad, the simple acoustic strains of her guitar an easy match for the din of the crowd. Even above the noise, there was a purity to her music that made it impossible not to listen, not to hear.

The hairs on the back of his neck stood on end, just as they had the first time he'd seen her, and out of nowhere, a thousand unwelcome memories rushed through him. That night, when he'd come to this very bar, in a foul mood, wanting to drown out the thoughts that persistently dogged him—of his failings and his guilt—and had seen Imogen for the very first time. She'd been singing, just like this, and her voice had done more than a succession of whiskies could: she'd been all he could focus on, a balm

unlike any he'd ever known. She'd been the birthday present he'd allowed himself, a moment of weakness in which
he'd surrendered to an animalistic need and passion, telling himself it would only be for one night.

Only he'd been wrong. The balm Imogen offered had
been addictive. Another night had followed, and another,
then many more, all tempestuous, overwhelmingly hot,
the kind of passion that had made him want more and
more, until he'd wondered if he'd ever get enough of Imogen Grant.

He'd had the knowledge in the back of his mind that it
had gone on too long, that he was wanting her too much,
almost coming to need her. As if she was some kind of
sorceress, making him think he deserved that sort of happiness when he knew that to be the last thing he could ever
enjoy, after what he'd done—or what he'd failed to do.

Luca had long carried the responsibility of his family's
deaths, and the guilt of that was something he would carry
for the rest of his life. So too his need for penance. Many
times, he'd wished he hadn't lived. He'd wished he'd died
alongside them and been spared from the fate of remembering his failures. But he hadn't, and so he'd committed to
the only path he considered viable: a life of sacrifice. A life
in which he went through the motions but astutely denied
himself any of the pleasures other people took for granted.

The morning she'd told him she loved him, he'd wanted
to stop the world spinning.

No, he'd wanted to scream. *You don't love me. You
can't. No one can.*

But instead, he'd broken up with her, ending it in such
a way to ensure she'd never want to see him again, because at that point, he'd known that was for the best—
for him, and for her. Not only did Luca refuse to allow

himself happiness, he knew he couldn't be trusted—not with another person's life. Not after what had happened to his parents and younger sister. He'd been responsible for their deaths—how could he ever trust himself not to make another fatal mistake, just like he had on that god-awful night? It was a risk too big to take—even if he thought he was worthy of her love.

Oh, he didn't doubt she'd loved him; Imogen was just that kind of person. Good and open, honest and emotionally available. A virgin when he'd met her, in more ways than one. While she'd been sexually inexperienced, he realised now she'd also been totally inexperienced with the world, and that had been part of the appeal. She was so different to the women he'd been with in the past, so unjaded, so uncynical. So easy and happy.

So warm.

Because he'd always gone for a certain type of woman before Imogen. Knowing the limitations of what he could offer, Luca had been careful to sleep with women who were as disinterested in a relationship as he was. Casual sex, very occasionally, was the most he was willing to allow for.

He dipped his head forward, staring at the amber liquid in his glass, willing it to flood his body with steel, to make him strong. He threw it back then turned slowly, bracing for the sight of Imogen, wondering if she would be very different. It had been almost three years—not long, really, but at the same time, going from twenty-two—which she'd been then—to twenty-five could bring about several changes in a woman's life.

She might be married now, for all he knew.

Even the turn towards the stage he executed with a mechanical slowness, as if to prove to himself every step of the way that he was in control.

And then he saw her, and he knew: he wanted her still. Three years hadn't changed that.

Her honey-brown hair was in some kind of braid, pulled over one shoulder and loose enough that tendrils had escaped on either side of her love-heart-shaped face, framing it like a piece of art. Her eyes were almond-shaped and wide-set, a caramel brown in colour. Her skin was tanned, covered in a dozen or so tiny freckles across the bridge of her nose and the top of her cheeks. Her lips, usually pale pink but painted a deep red tonight, were naturally a Cupid's bow shape. She closed her eyes as she sang, tapping one boot-clad foot against the bar of her stool, her fingers moving as if they were in a ballet, glancing across strings and somehow producing the kind of music that had the capacity to reach inside a person and fundamentally change them.

He stood perfectly still, hating her.

Hating her for the fact he still wanted her.

Hating her for the fact she'd ruined what they'd had by claiming to love him.

Hating her for reasons he couldn't even fathom.

And then he began to walk, his gait long and slow. He wore an immaculate jet-black suit and a crisp white shirt, his black hair combed back from his brow. He walked with the sort of energy that made people turn and look, even when they didn't realise he was one of the wealthiest men in the world. He stopped just short of the stage, his eyes holding to her with a steadiness that he couldn't fight.

She continued to sing, her eyes swept shut, her mouth moving in a way that was making his body tighten just watching her. More memories—her mouth, tentative at first, on his body, and by the end, so skilled at pressing his buttons, at knowing exactly what he liked, wanted, needed.

He suppressed a groan. She finished the song and smiled when the crowd applauded. Her eyes swept across the audience, briefly passing over him without showing even a hint of recognition and then, with a look of sheer terror, returning. He felt the emotions flooding through her even as he displayed none himself, even when he felt none.

Shock. Surprise. Anger. Resentment. Fury. Pain.

He had thought of her from time to time, had wondered if she'd forgiven him, then presumed not. He'd spoken to her in a way that was unforgivable. That had been his intention—and weirdly, at the time, it had been his pleasure. She had offered him something beautiful, something he'd known he didn't deserve, and so he'd taken a warped kind of pleasure in destroying it. He hadn't wanted to destroy Imogen, though; she'd been collateral damage. But if she'd created a fantasy of a life together, of being in a loving relationship with Luca, of loving him, then he had needed to annihilate that fantasy.

And so he had.

He saw now that she hadn't forgiven him.

Her fingers trembled almost imperceptibly as she reached for a glass of water, took a sip, then strummed the guitar. The crowd continued to buzz around them.

'Okay, guys,' she said, her speaking voice even more familiar than her singing. It was soft and husky, her accent British courtesy of having lived her whole life here in London. 'Just one more song to finish off. You'll probably recognise this one.'

She began to strum her guitar, the strains immediately

familiar—it had been a hit a couple years ago, a number one song by an American pop star you couldn't go any-where without hearing.

But in Imogen's hands, with her eyes practically cutting through Luca, the words could almost have been written for him. His lips twisted in a wry, mocking smile as she crooned the chorus,

And when the dawn light came
And the world started to glow golden
I saw you for what you really are
A man I'm not beholden
I saw you in all your glory
But glory's nothing to you
You're no one I want in my story.
I walked out, I stood tall
Next time I'll check before I fall.

Good. She should have checked before she'd fallen. And she was right about the glory thing too. Glory was nothing to him.

He'd presumed she'd known that about him, presumed she'd understood.

When he looked back, he wondered how the hell she'd ever thought she loved him. It was a testament to her goodness and nothing else. He'd made a point of restrict-ing their time together to bed. Conversation had been kept to a minimum. She'd been a month-long booty call, noth-ing more—and he'd been the same to her.

Or so he'd stupidly thought.

His hand formed a fist at his side as memories he went out of his way to suppress seemed to strangle him now. Her smile when she'd arrived at his place, the small gifts she'd brought. Things she'd noticed he didn't have but needed, foods she'd wanted him to try, the guitar she'd bought at a flea market and left there, because she often picked it up and played, simply because the spirit moved her. Weirdly, he still had it somewhere. The back of his wardrobe perhaps?

She sang the chorus again, and her eyes didn't leave his face. It hadn't been written for him, but it might as well have been, at least the way she was singing it.

She finished to rapturous applause, stood, bowed and went to walk off stage. He moved without thinking about it, his steps echoing her own, so that when she stepped into the crowd, he was there, his powerful body so much larger than her slim, petite frame.

Imogen was more than just beautiful; she was interesting. Her face had all the mystique of the Mona Lisa's. Her expressions were often hard to pin down; there was the sense that her brain was working all the time. It had kept him on his toes and had been part of her appeal. She dressed as she had then—like a musician—in a pair of skinny jeans, a loose singlet top with a silky wrap over her shoulders and a series of long chains around her slender neck, giving her an unmistakably bohemian vibe. He noticed without meaning to that she wore a selection of chunky rings on her fingers, but none bore a diamond and none were on her wedding finger.

'Excuse me,' she muttered, as if she didn't know him. As if they hadn't spent thirty nights in his bed, tangled in sheets and each other. As if he hadn't been her first lover. His body tightened at the memory.

He hadn't known.

He hadn't expected it.

If he'd known, he would have walked—no, run—away

from her. But she'd made a joke about it afterwards, as if it hadn't mattered, so he'd clung to that.

'A twenty-two-year-old virgin? Who woulda thunk it?'

'Imogen.' His voice emerged deep and raw. 'Let me buy you a drink.'

Her eyes widened and her lips parted. Hell, he was about three seconds away from pushing her against the wall and claiming that mouth with his own. He cursed inwardly, his whole body on fire.

'I can buy my own drink. I don't want anything from you.' She tilted her chin with defiance; he ached to reach out and stroke it with his thumb.

'Are you sure about that?'

She gasped again, glanced away.

'I'm meeting some friends,' she said after a beat.

'You sure you wouldn't rather meet me?'

And then, because he couldn't help himself, he shifted his hand, ever so slightly, so their fingers brushed and the familiar spark of awareness burst through him. As it did her. He saw it in the flush of her cheeks and the golden of her eyes.

She swallowed hard, her throat shifting visibly.

'I hope I *never* meet you again,' she said, with brutal honesty.

'I'm not so sure about that. I think you wish you felt that way, but in reality…'

'You don't know a damned thing about reality,' she volleyed back. Her eyes moved beyond him, and she smiled at someone over his shoulder. A tight smile, but it nonetheless changed her face in a way that made his gut roll, and for the briefest moment he was transported back to a time when she'd smiled for him. Not a tight, forced smile but a smile that radiated excitement and anticipation.

'I know that three years hasn't changed things between us,' he growled, dropping his head so he could whisper the words against her ear, his breath warm in the crook of her neck. He knew it drove her crazy and he felt her shiver in response. Power flooded his veins.

'Three years?' she managed to respond, but her voice trembled. 'Is that all it's been?'

He made a soft sound, a mocking half-laugh. 'You haven't missed me?'

'Like a hole in the head.'

She lifted her hand, perhaps intending to push him away, but instead, her fingers just stayed there, pressed to the crisp white of his shirt. Their bodies were so close, and as the pre-recorded music flooded the venue, the crowd grew louder and seemed to swarm around them, offering a level of anonymity he preferred.

'So you're not tempted to come home with me?'

Another gasp. 'Never.'

Still her hand was on his chest. He moved his hand to her hip, separating her singlet from her jeans so his fingers could brush the bare flesh at her side.

'It could be our secret. No one would need to know.'

'I would know.' She groaned though, as his hand moved around to her back and pushed her forward, so there was not even a whisper of space between his body and hers. He felt the moment she became aware of his arousal. Her eyes flew to his, her lips parted, her cheeks flushed pink.

'Or we could find somewhere here,' he suggested, lifting one brow, no longer on the fence about this at all. He wanted her. He needed her. Clearly he wasn't thinking straight, but it had always been this way with Imogen. She was a sorceress, but now that he knew that, he could control it. One night, one little misstep, and then he'd forget her again.

'Charming,' she ground out, but didn't move away from him. 'You're such a pig.'

'Something I thought you always understood about me.'

'Yeah, well, I didn't.'

'But now you do.' He dropped his lips to her jaw, kissing the flesh to the side of it, flicking her with his tongue so she trembled against his body. 'Don't we both deserve this?'

'I deserve so much better than this,' she responded, and he couldn't help but agree. She did—he didn't.

Let her go.

It would be the right thing to do. He couldn't toy with her. Couldn't destroy her again. He knew how badly he'd hurt her the first time, and while he'd been glad to get her out of his life, glad to remove her from his, to permanently remove the pleasure she'd given him, hurting her had been anathema to him. He didn't want to do that again.

But she was an enchantress—or perhaps it was just the chemistry they shared. There was something between them that was akin to a drug. He was like a recovering pseudo junkie, and now she was right in front of him, he needed a hit.

'Come home with me.'

Another soft groan. Of surrender?

'I'm meeting friends.'

It only strengthened his resolve. 'I'll wait.'

'I can't.'

'Of course you can.' He moved the hand at her back lower to cup her buttocks, holding her hard against his arousal. 'You know I'll make it worth your while.'

A small sob. A sound that he recognised as one of desperation—and surrender.

Power throbbed through him.

'Luca—'

Cristo. He loved it, how she said his name. He'd made millions of pounds before he turned twenty-one and had been a billionaire many times over before thirty, but it was the capitulation in Imogen's tone that truly made him feel as though he had won the lottery.

'Come home with me and let me hear you scream that,' he demanded.

'I hate you,' she whispered back, eyes huge when they met his.

'Good. I like hearing you say that much better than "I love you."'

She gasped. 'You are such a bastard.'

'This time, don't forget it.'

And with every last bit of willpower he possessed, he pulled away from her, waited a few seconds, then walked back to the bar, his long, easy stride concealing how much he wished he was still pressed hard against her beautiful body.

She was aware of him the whole time. As she went through the motions of catching up with friends, talking, laughing, she felt his eyes on her. He had stopped drinking alcohol. She noticed he held a bottle of mineral water in his hand as he watched her. Imogen sat on her single glass of wine all night. For hours.

She would usually have excused herself sooner, but she liked making him wait. She liked punishing him in some small way, even though she recognised that even *think-*

ing about going home with him was the stupidest thing she could ever do.

For so, so many reasons.

Her pulse fired as she replayed their relationship like a time capsule in her mind. The whirlwind nature of it all, how overwhelming it had been, how unprepared she'd been for someone like Luca, how naturally she'd viewed him through the prism of her own parents' long, happy marriage, how easily she'd believed they were falling in love with one another. How foolish she'd been! How rapidly she'd given him her heart, with no doubt that he'd welcome her proclamation of love and even return it. How devastating it had been when she'd told him she loved him and he'd laughed in her face.

The things he'd said that morning were a part of her now. They'd calcified inside her heart, forming lumps that were embedded in her psyche.

'You are a silly, naïve girl if you think this is love. We're sleeping together, not dating. You are not my girlfriend, and I am not your boyfriend. You're just someone I'm having sex with when I want to have sex. I could replace you in a heartbeat. No, I will *replace you in a heartbeat. Get out of my house.'*

She had felt physically sick. She had, in fact, vomited as soon as she'd walked out of his mansion. And then she'd vomited again the next morning. His words were still ringing in her ears, going around and around and around a week later, when she did a pregnancy test and realised she'd conceived their baby.

She paled now to think of Aurora, their beautiful daughter, at home with Imogen's twin sister, who looked after Aurora while Imogen worked. She thought of Aurora, the baby he most definitely wouldn't have wanted and didn't deserve, and knew she was playing with the kind of fire that would burn her badly if she wasn't careful. She couldn't let him find out about Aurora. The smart thing to do was run a mile from this man. He had broken her heart; hell, he'd broken *her*. For a very long time, all the light in her life had been extinguished. If it hadn't been for Aurora, she had no idea how she would have coped.

Yet his words were spinning through her mind, the things he'd said that awful morning like the laying down of a gauntlet she ached to pick up now. He'd been needlessly callous and utterly cruel, his cutting dismissal of her a wound she would never fully recover from. How could she not make him eat those words? He'd spoken to her as though nothing they'd shared had been special—yet here he was, three years later, clearly still attracted to her. She despised herself for needing that validation, and yet somehow, it mattered. Back then, Luca had been the one who'd called the shots, and she'd loved him too much to question it. But now? What if they could have this one night, and all on her terms? What if they could sleep together, only now, it would be Imogen who walked away—who made him feel worthless and easily replaceable?

Adrenaline sparked in her blood as she slid her empty glass across the table, stood up and excused herself from her friends. She glanced at Luca and then, without waiting to see if he followed, she walked out, aware that in a moment he would join her, and the juggernaut would start all over again.

Not really, though. This was not a juggernaut but rather an indulgence. A single step back in time for the one thing that had been good about them. Sex.

It had been almost three years for Imogen, and there was a fire in her blood that Luca had lit. She'd let him stoke it and extinguish it and then she'd have the satisfaction of walking away all over again. Because not only was he a selfish son of a bitch whom she hated with all her heart, he was also the father of a daughter he knew nothing about, and Imogen damn well intended for it to stay that way.

CHAPTER TWO

THEY HAD ONLY just got into his car when he reached for her, his mouth seeking hers, tasting her, as if he had been waiting for this moment his whole life. And she responded in kind, her body seeming to take on a life of its own as she climbed onto his lap, straddling him and kissing him until she could hardly breathe. His hands pushed through her hair, pulling it from the braid, and despite the jeans they both wore, his arousal pressed hard to her sex, making her moan as she rolled her hips with eager, desperate hunger for him.

He swore and she felt it in her soul, the same desperate, aching desire that was strangling her.

Three years. Had it really been so long? Kissing him now, it all felt so normal, so natural, as if they did this every night. Then again, he probably did. It wasn't like he was tucking a toddler into bed and reading them stories.

She had not a single doubt that she had done the right thing for her daughter by concealing her from Luca. Until she'd met Luca, she'd seen the world through rose-tinted glasses. At one point in time, the idea of keeping a father from his own child would have been anathema to her. But then she'd met Luca and she'd come face to face with a heart of darkness; she knew it had no place in Aurora's life.

She didn't want to think about that now. She couldn't help but feel conflicted even when she knew she'd done the best thing for everybody.

Fortunately, Luca made it very, very hard to think about anything, as his hand pushed at her singlet and found the lace of her bra, his thumb brushing over the fabric, teasing her nipple so she arched her back with a cry.

He made a guttural noise of agreement, and seconds later his head was under her singlet, his mouth on her breast, his tongue rolling her nipple through the bra so she was whimpering with a kind of euphoria that was all the more intense for how long it had been since she'd known anything like this.

Heaven help me, she thought, as he moved to the other breast and jerked his hips to drive his arousal harder against her sex. She dug down into the seat, needing to feel him, needing to be with him.

'How long until we're there?' she groaned, glancing at the window, not recognising where they were.

'Too long,' he snapped back, the words imbued with as much desperation as she felt. Then he swore, pulled his head out of her shirt and sought her mouth once more, kissing her like his survival hung in the balance, kissing her hard and hungrily—angrily too. It was an anger she totally understood.

She was furious with herself for doing this, for wanting him. Furious with herself for being weak.

This man was lava, or quicksand. Dangerous. Bad for her. She knew that, and she knew she should avoid him like the plague, and yet it had taken Luca a mere three minutes to convince her to go home with him. Where was her sanity? Where was her self-preservation?

But this wouldn't be like last time. She was stronger now. She understood better.

Her childish idealism had been trampled, replaced with a lens of gritty reality. At least when it came to Luca Romano.

After what felt like an eternity, the car turned into the alleyway behind his mansion and the garage gate drew up. The driver manoeuvred the SUV in and cut the engine.

Luca moved quickly, easing Imogen off his lap as he opened the door and stepped out, his arousal obvious courtesy of the fit of his suit. The lights were fluorescent—a metaphorical bucket of water—but such a thing had no power to lessen her need for him.

Imogen half stepped out of the car and he half lifted her, throwing her over his shoulder and carrying her from the garage in the most expedient way possible.

'I can walk, you know,' she said gruffly, but his hand had curved around her bottom and her whole body was trembling with need, so she wasn't even sure if her statement was accurate.

'Do you want to?'

She hated him. She hated him for knowing her weakness, for knowing the depth of her need; she hated him so much and for so many reasons.

The house was instantly familiar, bringing back a thousand different memories, memories she wished to avoid.

But it also brought with it realisations. Time had elapsed. She'd grown older and a hell of a lot wiser. She'd never been here in the daylight. Not for longer than it took her to evacuate in the mornings. He'd never offered for her to stay when he was leaving for work, and he left early.

In the evenings, they'd spend the night in some kind of wonderful thrall and then it would be over again.

How had she missed the fact it had just been sex for him?

She'd been so naïve.

They were just inside the lounge room when he eased her to the floor and started kissing her again. This time his powerful, strong hands stripped her clothes as he went, one by one, removing her shawl, her singlet, her bra. While she kicked out of her boots, he unfastened her jeans and pushed them down, his hands brushing her bare thighs as she stepped out of the fabric. Her hands pushed at his jacket as he removed her underwear, and then he was drawing a condom from his wallet as he unfastened his belt and trousers, then slid them down just enough to sheath himself. He lifted her with a deep, rough groan, the kind of sound she could never emulate because it was so masculine and so uniquely *Luca*. He thrust into her as he held her around his waist, the groan exploding into the room as he filled her more completely than he ever had before.

Or perhaps it was just his absence that had made her feel that way. Maybe it had always been like this, but she'd been in such a fog of fantasy land, thinking it would last for ever, that she hadn't completely appreciated how mind-blowing it was to be with him.

He stepped forward so her back was against a wall, and with each thrust she felt her sanity spiralling, her need growing, her passion exploding, so when she came it was like all the molecules in the universe were being rearranged, rebuilt, overbright and overlarge.

'Luca.' She cried his name, just as he'd said she would, and she didn't stop there. She called it over and over again, as he drove into her until her eyes were filled with a firestorm of lights and her whole body was singing. She dropped her head onto his shoulder in a sign of total and utter surrender, her body wrapped around his like a vine. Sweat sheened her body, and his. She was no longer conscious of where he began and she ended.

Heat licked the soles of her feet.

He began to move, carrying her deeper into the house, to his room, where he placed her on the bed.

Ghosts lingered here.

Ghosts of the kind of pleasure that was impossible to define. And the kind of pain that could almost kill a person. She ignored the latter. She didn't want to think of that now. Not when he was moving inside of her again, his powerful, strong body over hers. She realised, belatedly, that he was still dressed, and her hands moved impatiently to shove his shirt off his body, but the buttons were hard and her fingers hardly co-operated.

But somehow it felt important to be naked with him, a levelling experience of intimacy, a need to see that he had surrendered as much as she had. She grunted as she pushed at his shirt, breaking several buttons from the stitching, earning a gruff sound of amusement.

'I would have helped, if you'd asked.'

'I don't feel like asking,' she responded, shoving at his pants next. But this time, he helped, pulling away from her just long enough to push his own clothes off before returning to her.

'What do you feel like?'

'Isn't it obvious?'

'Tell me what you want.' His commanding tone sent shivers down her spine, shivers of need and desire.

'This.'

'No. Be specific.'

Heat flushed her cheeks. He was taunting her. He knew she was shy. He knew she was innocent and inexperienced.

'You are not a twenty-two-year-old virgin any more. You've been with other men, learned things. So? What do you like? What's changed?'

She was suddenly completely still.

She *hadn't* been with other men, as a point of fact. She'd been a little busy growing their baby then caring for her, but his easy supposition that her life had been a whirlwind string of affairs highlighted what his own had been like.

'I could replace you in a heartbeat.'

How many women had been in this bed since her?

Ice flooded her veins and she was momentarily stiff, cold, aching all over, just like she had back then.

'Imogen.' Only, his voice was a warm caress, bringing her back to the moment, to pleasure and passion. She closed her eyes, refusing to think about the past, his other women, about anything but this. Because she knew one thing for damned sure: when the morning came and dawn light broke, she would walk away from him, and this time it would be for good. Her small slice of payback. Childish, perhaps, but important to Imogen.

'I want this. One night of meaningless, amazing sex, and then I want to forget you even exist, you bastard.'

His smile almost looked to be one of relief. 'Excellent. That I can do.'

He was glad the next morning when he woke to find her gone. Glad that there was no need for a conversation about the past, for a conversation of any sort. He was glad that she hadn't stayed, even when his body still yearned for her, and he knew he would have liked one more chance to be with her before she'd left.

Had she left in the early hours of the morning, or once he'd fallen asleep? He had no recollection beyond their multiple comings together. He remembered making love to her until her voice was hoarse and her body spent. He remembered kissing her all over, pinning her arms above her head, delighting in the way his body could so easily master hers, even when the flipside was an uneasy dominance she held over him too. How one simple touch from her could drive him wild. He remembered her taking his length in her mouth as though she'd been fantasising about it for years, her eyes lifting to his as she took him deep, his hands curving around her head, touching her without driving her motions, needing some air of control though because his body was being shredded by what she could do to him.

It had been a perfect, sublime night. An excellent birthday present to himself, on his thirty-third birthday. And this from a man who never celebrated the passage of time. For each year he grew older was another year further from when his family had been alive. Each year he lived was a marked reminder that they had not. And that he had been to blame.

His fingers ran over his scarred side distractedly, the marks he bore a welcome, constant reminder of how he'd failed his mother, father and little sister, Angelica.

There was a new mark above his hip bone. A purple bruise. A hickey, he realised, recalling Imogen's lips pressed there, while her hands worked the rest of his body, his arousal, until he was calling her name, reaching for her hips, positioning her on his length and taking her from underneath, staring up at her breasts as she rolled her hips and tormented him with the perfection of her tightness.

He swore loudly into the bathroom, his gaze meeting its reflection in the mirror, as he acknowledged to himself, and only for a moment, what a liar he was.

He was *not* glad she was gone.

He would have endured any number of conversations if it meant he could screw her one last time.

'I want to have meaningless, amazing sex, and then I want to forget you even exist.'

He closed his eyes.

'You bastard.'

Fair enough. He was better to take her approach to this, and let sleeping dogs lie. He knew what would happen if he saw her again.

They'd fall back into bed together.

Again.

And again.

And again.

But to what end?

Imogen hated him now, but she'd loved him once and he couldn't risk that she might do so again. He didn't want anything like that kind of complication. He shuddered at the thought. Imogen Grant was now firmly, well and truly, a part of his past life, and that was that.

At least, it should have been, but evidently, this was not the case. Not even three nights after his birthday, he found himself at the same bar, listening to Imogen once more, his whole body on fire with a need for her he couldn't ignore, even when he knew he really should.

She wore a long floaty dress and a heap of bangles that jangled prettily as she strummed the guitar. She sang as though the words had been dug from her soul, the ballad not one he knew but one he found instantly catchy. The crowd was mesmerised; such was her appeal. When she stood up to walk off stage, he left his place at the bar and strode towards her. She stepped down, not seeing him, walking towards another man instead.

He stopped walking, his gut twisting at the sight of her natural, full smile, at the way she pulled her hair over one shoulder before wrapping her arms around the man's waist and laughing at something he said. She punched his shoulder playfully—flirtingly—and Luca's body turned to stone.

The man leaned closer, whispered something. She looked up at him, nodded. He put a hand in the small of her back, guided her away, towards a table. Unlike the other night, there was no group of friends waiting for her. This was more intimate. A date.

His body went from ice-cold to red-hot.

So, what did he expect?

Obviously, she'd been with other guys since him. Obviously, she had no reason to not be seeing someone tonight. Never mind that it had only been a few nights since they'd slept together. What did that matter?

She was a free agent, and the sex had been meaningless. Right?

He stalked back to the bar, threw down some notes, grabbed his jacket and left, determined not to think of her again.

'It's not a recording contract or anything,' Imogen said with a shake of her head, trying to contain Gen's excitement. 'It's just an invitation to send a demo.'

'From the head of a label,' Gen exclaimed. 'Hel-*lo*. That's amazing. Why are you downplaying this?'

Because Imogen had learned not to count her chickens before they hatched. Because she'd learned to keep both feet firmly planted in reality, to not trust how things appeared. 'Until there's a signed contract, I'm just seeing this for what it is—an opportunity.'

'Come on, Immi. After that song, everyone wants a piece of you.'

'That's so not true. I've had some songwriting offers, but you know that's not my dream.'

'Right. *This* is your dream. And you're there, baby. They want you.'

Imogen rolled her eyes.

'Higher. More high!'

She turned back to Aurora who was on a swing, buckled in place, and had been enjoying the sensation of jettisoning through the air until her mummy and aunt had become so locked in conversation they'd stopped swinging her altogether.

Imogen gave the back of the swing a push, smiling as Aurora's chubby legs, encased in hot pink leggings, swung wildly through the air.

'They want me to submit a demo. Along with, probably, hundreds of other aspiring singers.'

'No one is as talented as you.'

'I'm not saying I'm not happy,' she conceded after a beat. 'I'm just being pragmatic. There's a heap of things that need to line up before I get a recording contract. This is just one step in a very long path.'

'But it is a step,' Gen said, batting her lashes with the kind of optimism Imogen had once had in spades.

'Yeah,' she conceded after a beat. 'It's a step.'

'Right.' Gen nodded approvingly. 'I have to love and leave you beautiful people. I've got a date.'

Imogen wrinkled her nose. 'Who is it today? Da Vinci or van Gogh?'

'Both, if there's time. You know I don't play favourites.'

Imogen hugged her sister, watching as she walked away from the playground and towards the tube, which would take her to the National Gallery. Where Imogen was fluent in all forms of music and had been for almost as long as she could walk, Genevieve adored art and spent every spare moment she had studying paints and portraits. It didn't matter how many times she looked at the same pieces, she swore that they conveyed different things to her each time. Her obsession would have been hard to understand were it not for the fact Imogen was someone who read scores as if they were novels.

'See you tonight. I'll make butter chicken.'

'Baba chimiken!' Aurora repeated, clapping her little hands together and tilting her head back. 'Buh-bye, Gen-Gen!'

Genevieve blew several kisses, waved and continued to walk away.

Despite the approach of winter, the day was clear and, in the sun, warm enough to enjoy, so they stayed at the park longer than Imogen had intended. After a while, though, Aurora began to flag. Imogen scooped her up and placed her in the stroller, walking towards a nearby café to grab a fortifying coffee for the tube ride home.

While there were several playgrounds closer to their home, this particular place had become a favourite. Not only was it huge, it was also fenced, close to Gen's work, and more often than not, there were several other children playing there, meaning Aurora could busy herself making toddler talk with them. Besides, they quite enjoyed the tube trip there and back—Aurora loved to ride the 'fast trainies.'

Stifling a yawn, Imogen pushed into a busy café, stroking the soft brown hair on Aurora's head as she joined the queue to order her coffee. She was about five people deep and while she waited, she thought about the songs she'd play at the bar next time, the students she was teaching piano, the pieces she was working on. She thought about anything, in fact, besides Luca.

His touch had been a betrayal of everything she'd sworn to herself. She was furious with herself, not least of all because it truly had exposed her to weakness.

She'd been doing *fine*. She'd been *over him*. She barely thought of him any more, except when Aurora pulled a certain face or looked at her with those intelligent brown eyes and she'd see right through their daughter to the soul of her father. But other than that, Luca had been out of her life and mind. And now he wasn't. Now he was the last thing she thought of at night and the first thing she thought of in the morning. Now he was back to being a source of torment and torture and she was so damned mad at herself. How could she have been so stupid as to think she could sleep with him and walk away, as though he meant nothing to her? No matter how much she wished that were true, it would never be the case. She might hate him, but she simply couldn't forget him—it was a curse she had to live with.

At the front of the line, she ordered her drink, then moved to the side to wait for it. Aurora was babbling, a sign that she was close to sleep. Imogen crouched down and spoke to her instead. She used Aurora's nap time—in the middle of the day—to work, and if Aurora fell asleep now, she wouldn't nap later. So, Imogen engaged the toddler with little sing-songs and nursery rhymes until the coffee was ready and her name was called.

'Imogen? Double shot oat cap with vanilla syrup for Imogen?'

It wasn't an uncommon name. There were undoubtedly many women who shared it. But for some reason, Luca glanced up when he heard the call, his own double shot espresso sitting on the edge of his papers.

And then, he saw her.

Unmistakably Imogen, but as he'd never seen her before. This was Daytime Imogen, not dressed to perform, but casually, comfortably, in leggings, an oversized T-shirt and a puffer jacket that did nothing to hide her fragile beauty. He couldn't stop staring. She reached for her coffee on the edge of the bar, her face lighting up as she smiled at the barista then turned her attention lower.

To something.

A pram.

A stroller.

And someone.

His gut twisted; he stood without realising it.

Was she babysitting? Or was she a mother now?

He hadn't expected that, but why not? What did he really know about her life, then or now? Hadn't he gone out of his way *not* to know about her?

He watched as she pushed out of the café, coffee in hand, talking to the occupant of the stroller the whole way, and he followed behind, as if drawn by some invisible thread. She turned in the direction of the tube station, then she was almost level with his own car, double parked on the sidewalk while he took a quick meeting.

But Imogen was not as fast as Luca. He walked quickly and, when he was at her back, said her name. Softly, but that didn't matter. She turned around, the guilt in her face impossible to miss.

'*You!*' she cried accusingly, her face pale. 'What the hell are you doing here? Are you *following* me?'

It was a ridiculous assertion. 'Like I have nothing better to do with my time,' he responded gruffly. 'I just finished a meeting around the corner, grabbed a coffee, and then I saw you.'

'Oh, right.' She pressed a hand to her forehead, drawing in a quick breath. 'Of course.'

But there was a stroller in front of her with a little high-pitched voice emerging from it endlessly.

'Anyway, I have to get going.'

'Where to?'

'Um, that's none of your business.'

Her usual bravado was gone, though—robbed by the surprise of seeing him, he suspected.

'Imogen, what's going on?'

'Nothing, I'm just— I have to go.' She turned away from him, began to walk again, faster now. Something was shifting inside of him. He should have just let her go—Imogen's life was her business, and not his, but there was the strangest sense inside of him, an instinct he had always trusted, that there was more going on than he realised.

'Mummy, dog! Dog! Stop, dog!' the occupant of the stroller called as a woman walked past with a little West Highland terrier.

Luca's footing faltered. He stopped walking, his lungs burning as he drew in a breath. He was very, very rarely surprised, but that made twice in his life Imogen had managed to pull the rug out from under him. Once, when she'd claimed to love him. And now, discovering she'd had a child. With whom? And when? And why did it matter? She was just some woman he'd slept with a million years ago. She was nothing to him. *Niente.*

'Imogen, stop.'

'Why?' She kept walking. In fact, she sped up, so she was almost running. He increased his own pace, then caught her arm.

'Is it some great secret?' he demanded. 'You don't want me to meet your child?'

She stared at him with such wide eyes and such *fear* that his instincts kicked into overdrive again. There was something going on here. Something he had to understand.

With a last glance at her pinched, pale face, he moved around the stroller so he could see the child for himself.

He almost passed out. Sitting there, beaming out at the world, with dark, dark eyes and soft brown ringlets, was a toddler who was the spitting image of his little baby sister, Angelica, a child he hadn't seen in twenty-one long years.

And he knew.

He knew in that way one simply knows the incontrovertible facts of life that the little girl sitting in the stroller smiling up at him was his daughter.

He had a child.

He was a father.

And he wished, with all his heart and every fibre of his soul, that it was not the case.

CHAPTER THREE

'You're sure you can't at least eat before you go?' Gen's voice showed clear concern.

Eat? As if. Imogen felt as if her stomach was tied in so many knots it would never be able to accommodate food again.

'I'll grab something while I'm out,' she lied, amazed that her voice emerged mostly normal sounding. She cleared her throat to conceal the slight tremor. Inwardly, she couldn't stop shaking.

'We will discuss this tonight, Imogen, and that is non-negotiable.'

He'd spoken in a tone she'd never heard, reminding her forcefully of how much she didn't know about Luca. For all they'd spent a month together, three years ago, she had realised subsequently how much of himself he'd kept from her. She'd spoken freely about her life, her aspirations, her thoughts, her dreams and hopes, but he had revealed so very little, and what he had shared had been like pulling teeth.

She knew that he worked tirelessly, that he played to win, was super successful, and yes, she knew that he was ruthless. Even without the way he'd treated her, she'd understood that.

'But you went to so much trouble and it smells *so* good,' Gen said, eyeing the butter chicken, naan bread and pilaf.

'So good.' Aurora smacked her hand to the tray of her high chair. Genevieve smiled indulgently.

'If I'm hungry, I'll eat when I get home.'

'I doubt Missy here will leave any leftovers,' Gen quipped, and Imogen smiled, but it felt forced. She could hardly think straight.

'Okay, call if you need anything. I won't be late.'

'Don't rush back. We've got a scintillating marathon of *Bluey* awaiting us after dinner, and then an early night.'

'You're the best.' She pressed a kiss to her sister's cheek and then to Aurora's head, breathing in the little girl with a strange feeling in her chest. She knew what caused the sensation. As she pulled the front door of their flat closed, she admitted that she was hovering on a precipice. Behind her was the old world, the one with which she was familiar and comfortable, and which she'd made work for her. But with each step she took away from their flat, their home, from her sister and daughter, with each step she took closer to Luca's, she acknowledged she was travelling further into something new and terrifying.

He knew about Aurora.

He knew that she'd had his baby, and that she hadn't told him. He knew that they were parents. He knew the bare minimum at this stage, because he'd peppered her with questions once he'd realised, and she'd answered in a state of total shock.

What was her name? How old was she? Was she healthy? What was she like?

She had no clue what he'd do with that information, but at the very least, he wanted more answers than she could have given him standing on the footpath outside a busy café.

Her mind was every bit as knotted as her stomach. She rode the tube to Sloane Square, then walked the short distance to his house, her heart steadily palpitating its way to her throat with each step she took.

At the door, she could barely bring herself to press the buzzer. It would bring about the crossing of a line from which there was no return.

But she had to do it. There was no escaping this and she wasn't a coward. She couldn't hide from him indefinitely. Not now he knew. Not when he had all the resources he did at his disposal. There was nowhere she could go that he wouldn't find her.

Fidgeting her fingers, she forced herself to ring his doorbell then took a sharp step backwards, as if to immediately put space between herself and the conversation that had to take place. She heard his footsteps, felt the whooshing inwards of the door, then saw him on the other side and wanted to throttle herself and her traitorous body for responding to him on a physical level. Just one sight of him and her pulse went thready for a whole other reason.

This was *not* the time to think about that.

She swallowed hard, forcing herself to focus.

He gestured silently for her to enter. She did so, careful not to brush close to him as she crossed the threshold. He noticed and gave her a mocking arch of his brow.

She wanted to punch him.

'So?' She shrugged out of her coat, hanging it on a hook by the door, turning back to him in time to catch the last flicker of his gaze travelling the length of her body. She shivered. She'd worn a black blouse that was buttoned up to the throat with a frilly collar in a sort of turn-of-the-century bohemian vibe, tucked into tailored jeans, and ballet flats. Hardly seductive, but the way she caught him looking at her sent her pulse rate skyrocketing.

'We need to talk,' he muttered, gesturing towards the lounge room.

She eyed it suspiciously before stepping through the wide doors, remembering the last time she'd been here and they'd made love against the wall, unable to wait until his bedroom.

She studiously avoided that area of the room, choosing instead to focus on the plush leather armchairs. He moved past her, towards a sleek cabinet that housed a liquor cabinet and inbuilt fridge, opening it and removing the bottle of wine that she'd always loved.

Was that a thoughtful gesture or just a coincidence? Definitely the latter. He poured her a glass then walked back to her.

'Drink this before you pass out.'

'I'm fine.'

'You don't look fine.'

Her heart dropped to her toes. Had he been looking at her with sympathy rather than admiration?

'Well, whose fault is that?'

'Do you really want to start talking about blame, Imogen?' he demanded, so she felt the full force of his emotions rioting towards her. 'I have a daughter I knew nothing about until today. A daughter I never would have found out about were it not for pure chance.'

She swallowed hard, fidgeting her spare hand and then taking a gulp of wine. Suddenly her nerves were in disarray and it was the only way she could think of to calm them.

'I'm more than happy to talk about blame,' she responded tautly. 'What could I do, Luca? After the way things ended between us, when I found out I was pregnant, I didn't even think of coming to you. You'd made it abundantly clear what I meant to you, and what you wanted from me. It definitely wasn't to become parents together.'

A muscle jerked in his jaw; his eyes bore into hers. 'That was about you and me,' he said, slashing his hand through the air. 'The moment you found out you were pregnant, I should have found out too.'

'Why?'

'Decency? Courtesy? Respect?'

'All of which you showed me so much of, right?'

'So, was this some sick kind of revenge? This is a child's life, a parent's place in their life. You toyed with both of us.'

'How dare you?' she shouted, quickly taking another gulp of wine and rejoicing in the fire it lit on its way down her throat. 'You have no right to say that to me. I am a damned good mother. I give her *everything*. You stand there and act all holier-than-thou, when perhaps you should be asking yourself how many other kids you have out there.'

He put a hand on his hip. 'I am *always* careful.'

'Yeah? What's your point? We were always careful, and I still got pregnant.'

'You weren't on the pill.'

'So, you're blaming me?'

He closed his eyes in a wave of visible frustration. 'It's an extra precaution I'd presumed was in place.'

'Given that I'd never had sex, I'd had no need for contraception.'

His nostrils flared. 'There's no point discussing the "why" of this. It happened. You got pregnant. I'm more interested in how you justified your decision. Why keep it a secret from me?'

'I didn't keep it a secret from you,' she hissed. 'You weren't in my life. You were nowhere.' Her voice broke a little. She hated that. She hated the emotion he could still bring to the fore, even when she despised him. 'But I knew you wouldn't want her. I did you a favour, Luca.'

'Do not—' he spoke quietly, calmly, yet she could feel his anger pulsing towards her '—presume to tell me how I would have felt.'

'Oh, come on,' she said with a humourless laugh. 'We were both there. You made it abundantly clear what your priorities were in life. As if you would have wanted to be a father.'

'Whether I wished it or not, you were pregnant. I should have known that, and I should have known our daughter before today.'

Her stomach rolled. Was he right? Had she made the wrong decision?

Not when she considered the way he'd spoken to her. It hadn't been about them as a couple; it hadn't been about revenge, or wanting to hurt him or withhold their child from him. It had been about wanting to protect their daughter as much as anything.

'I didn't trust you,' she admitted slowly. 'I *don't* trust you.'

'What does that mean?'

'You're cruel, Luca.'

He flinched a little, but concealed it quickly.

'I was so caught up in you at first, I didn't understand. I didn't see it. I was overwhelmed by the whole sex thing. But you're a bastard, cold and unfeeling and capable of

using people for your own ends. Honestly, we were just…
better off without you.'

She threw the words at him but didn't feel any pleasure in saying them. They hurt to say, in fact. She blinked
quickly, to clear the sting of tears.

His only reaction was to take a step closer, reach for
her wine glass and take a sip before returning it to her.

'I don't disagree.'

Her eyes widened and she tamped down on an immediate reflexive response of contradiction.

'Unfortunately, we're stuck with one another now.'

She closed her eyes in a wave of uncertainty. A bad
moon was rising, and she didn't know how to deal with it.

'What does that mean?' It was her turn to sip.

He pressed a finger to her chin, tilting her face, and
when she opened her eyes, she was staring right at him.

'If I could choose, I would choose not to have children.
I have never wanted that.' His voice was cold, emotionless.
'But she is here—a real person, my daughter.' A hint of
feeling darkened his words, but he smothered it quickly.
'I have no choice but to be a part of her life.'

Imogen flinched.

It was her very worst nightmare. How could Luca be a
part of Aurora's life without being a part of *her* life too?

She groaned, shaking her head a little. 'It's not possible. It would be too confusing to her. She has no idea
who you are.'

'And why is that?'

Imogen's knees felt wobbly. She gripped the wine glass
harder.

'You have one option here, though perhaps you cannot see that.'

Wariness crept along her spine.

'I will tell you what I want, and you will agree. It would not be wise to fight me on this.'

Imogen blinked up at Luca, seeing the steel in his features, and she baulked. She knew he was cold, and she knew what he was capable of, but in her heart of hearts, she had still clung to the notion that there was some goodness in him, somewhere.

She had to believe that—he was a part of their daughter's DNA, and darling Aurora was all sunshine and light.

'Is that a threat?'

His eyes bore into hers, almost seeing through her. 'Threats tend to be idle. What I am saying is not.'

She shivered. 'And what exactly are you saying?'

He was so close she could feel his warm breath against her temple as he exhaled. 'I want custody of her.'

Imogen gasped. 'You can't be serious.'

'Not sole custody,' he said, as though that made any difference. 'But she is my daughter. I demand legal recognition of that fact.'

'You *demand*?' she repeated, incensed. 'You just said you don't want to be a father—'

'But I am.'

Imogen swallowed, shaking her head a little. Not because she was rejecting his demand, but because she couldn't process it.

'I have a daughter I knew nothing about,' he said, the words flooded with a strange, almost far-away emotion.

'I know.' What more could she say?

'I want her here, under my roof.'

Imogen gasped, her headshake becoming more determined. 'She has a home, with me…'

'And I recognise that it would be cruel to separate the

two of you—at this stage, at least. Unfortunately, that means you will have to be a part of this.'

Her stomach clenched at the obvious displeasure he took in suggesting any such thing. He could not make it any clearer that having Imogen was the last thing he wanted. Why did that hurt so much, even now? She had to take back control of this conversation, to reassert her independence.

'No.' She shook her head quickly, dislodging his finger from her chin. 'No *way*.'

'You're not listening to me,' he interrupted. 'She is *our* daughter, and *we* will raise her.'

'If you want to be a part of her life, you can be, but I'm sure as hell not living with you.' Her whole body felt as if it were filled with an electrical current at the very idea.

'Let me say this more clearly. I would like us to come to an agreement, but if you will not be reasonable, I have a meeting with a lawyer tomorrow morning and you had better believe I'll get access to our daughter through the courts. It will not be in her best interests, but I will fight you for what should always have been mine, Imogen.'

She was trembling so much she thought she might fall. She stepped backwards and backwards again, collapsing into one of the armchairs and clasping the wine glass in her lap. She stared straight ahead, her whole life flashing before her eyes, everything wonky and aching.

She couldn't fight him.

She didn't have the resources. While she and Gen were doing okay, and her parents were comfortable, no one was in a position to bankroll the kind of legal fight she had no doubt Luca would launch.

'She's my daughter,' Imogen whispered.

She wasn't even aware of the tears that were falling

down her cheeks until Luca appeared at her side, holding a tissue. Instead of passing it to her, he wiped her cheeks with surprising gentleness.

'Yes. I'm aware of that, and I have no interest in taking her away from you, even when I can see that would probably be fair retribution for the fact you took her away from me.'

Imogen tried to suck in air but struggled.

'I am asking you to live here, with her, for a while. I am asking you to be reasonable and see this from my perspective. I have a daughter I just found out about. Don't I deserve a chance to get to know her? And wouldn't that be easier for her if you were a part of it?'

Luca stared at the wall without seeing. Their conversation was replaying in his mind like a film, every word, every sentence.

Every threat.

He dropped his head forward, staring at the floor, breath burning in his lungs.

Yes, he'd threatened her. He'd been so damned angry, so utterly shocked—at Imogen, as well as himself. Why hadn't it occurred to him that she might be pregnant? They'd slept together for a month, and before that, she'd been innocent. Hadn't it been foreseeable that there were consequences of their time together?

He clenched his teeth, trying to put himself back into the mind-set he'd had then. He'd been furious with her for loving him, furious with himself for letting it go so far, and he'd been missing her.

Missing her more than he'd allowed himself to admit...

Now, though, this wasn't about Imogen. It wasn't about

his need for her, or her desire for him. None of that mattered any more. He was a father.

His gut rolled, and images of his own father populated his brain, almost driving him to despair. His own father had been the very best of men. He'd been a behemoth, a pillar of morality, intelligence, strength and good humour. He had stood like a beacon to Luca, a guide, always, as to how he should act—and Luca had failed him.

He couldn't fail his daughter—if only because Luca could finally do something which might, in some small part, atone for the mistakes of his past.

But what if he *did* fail her? What if he made a mistake again? What if he hurt her?

Panic stole through him, a familiar heat flooding through his veins so he couldn't think straight, and his breathing grew rushed.

He was not a twelve-year-old boy any more, though. The mistake of that night had been borne of his immaturity, his selfishness. Now Luca was a grown man, and he would give his life for Aurora's, in a heartbeat. He would move heaven and earth to keep her safe, to protect her. Though he'd never wanted to be a father, now that he was, he had no choice but to be the best damned father that little girl could have. Even if it meant having Imogen in the mix as well…

A scowl marred his face as he imagined what that might look like. Imogen was the one woman who'd ever weakened his resolve and got under his skin; she was the one woman who'd made him stray from his commitment to a lonely life of constant self-flagellation to atone for his guilt. In the past, he'd been weak, but he couldn't let that happen again.

He would keep her at arm's length this time around, even if the effort nearly killed him.

* * *

'You're *moving out*?' Genevieve whispered over a steaming cup of tea later that night.

Imogen grimaced, nodding. 'I can't see an alternative.'

'Run away,' Genevieve muttered, only half joking. 'Immi, listen. You didn't tell me the gory details, but you didn't need to. I know what this guy did to you. I *saw* what he did to you. I heard the goddamned songs you wrote. He *broke* you.'

Imogen closed her eyes on a wave of remembering. It had been bad. Very, very bad.

'He's her father. He has rights.'

'To see her, sure. But not to make you move in with him. What kind of sick control move is that?'

'Believe it or not, he's trying to do what's best for her. He wants to make up for lost time…'

Genevieve snorted, then placed her tea on the counter, her features rearranging themselves into a mask of serious contemplation. 'Listen, Im. You cannot do that with this guy.'

'Do what?'

'See the best in him.' Genevieve cupped Imogen's hands and lifted them to her chest. 'I know that's your default position, but not with him. Don't you dare let your guard down around this guy, or I'll never forgive you.'

'If I let my guard around him, I'll never forgive myself.' She squeezed Genevieve's hands. 'Try not to worry. We'll see you all the time; I'm just a few tube stops away.'

When Luca arrived the next day to collect Imogen and Aurora, she realised he'd worked fast. Somehow he'd had a car seat installed in his Range Rover, and the back pockets were stuffed with nappies, kids' books and rattles.

She tried not to let that endear him to her.

She was conscious, as she carried her suitcase to the door, of Genevieve's disapproving, arctic scowl.

'Im? Call me when you get there.'

'I'll be fine,' Imogen assured her sister. Then, belatedly, as Luca went to retrieve her luggage, she said, 'Genevieve, this is Luca. Luca, my twin sister.'

Luca went to extend his hand to shake but Genevieve glared at it as though he was holding a slither of snakes.

'Listen to me,' she muttered, moving close enough that a nearby Aurora wouldn't hear. 'You had better be nice, or so help me God, I will…do something. You don't deserve this,' she gestured to Imogen and then Aurora.

His eyes darkened and Imogen felt his surprise, but it just made her love her sister all the more. She reached across and squeezed Genevieve's arm. 'I'll be fine. I've got this.' She could only pray that was true.

Genevieve nodded once, smiled at her sister, hugged her, then scooped Aurora off the ground. She kissed the toddler's head, Genevieve's eyes a little misty as she passed the girl to Imogen.

'I can see my reputation precedes me,' Luca drawled, as Imogen clipped Aurora into the car seat then took her own seat beside him.

'What did you expect? A bed of roses?'

'I didn't expect anything,' he returned, pulling the car into traffic. She sat back in her seat, staring moodily through her own window without really seeing. He drove the busy London streets expertly, as she suspected he did all things in his life—except for relationships.

'Do you have any friends?'

He shifted a sidelong glance at her. 'Why do you ask?'

Deflection. She hadn't recognised his techniques three

years ago—she'd been too mired in the fog of their chemistry to analyse anything very deeply—but she saw them
now. He was nudging the conversation away, not answering her question but disguising that with interest in her.
It had worked in the past. Now it frustrated her, but she
didn't show it.

'Because you're such a charmer, of course,' she responded with a lift of one shoulder. Before turning back
to her window, she saw the way his knuckles morphed
into a shade of white, as if gripping the steering wheel
very tightly.

They travelled the rest of the way in silence, except for
Aurora's occasional babbling sounds from the back seat.
Happy babbling, because Aurora was almost always smiling and shining. Imogen hoped that would continue to be
the case. She gnawed on her lower lip as they travelled,
until he pulled into the familiar alley that provided rear
access to his home, pressing a button so the garage door
opened seamlessly, and the car slipped in. Briefly she was
reminded of the other night, when they'd come to his home
and passion had been thick in the air between them. Now
it was tension, so awful that it could be cut with a knife.

He went to the rear door, to lift out Aurora, but Aurora glanced at him then Imogen. 'Mama.' She pointed
at Imogen. 'Want Mama.'

Imogen saw the accusing look in his eyes, but he took
a step back, saying nothing to Aurora or Imogen. She felt
what he would have said, though. She felt the blame and
recriminations, and the certainty she'd once felt, that she
had done the right thing by keeping Aurora from him,
took a slight tumble.

With a reassuring smile at Aurora, she unclipped her
and put their daughter on her hip, walking around the car

towards the door. Luca had grabbed some luggage and was holding it, staring straight ahead, his shoulders tense. His whole body radiated stress. Anger?

Probably a whole host of emotions. This time yesterday, he'd had no idea about Aurora, and now he was moving her—and Imogen—in to live with him.

The moment they crossed the threshold from the garage to his home, she recognised just how busy he—or an army of minions—had been. The changes were subtle but noticeable to Imogen. All of the breakable artsy pieces had been moved from the coffee tables and low-lying shelves. Small plastic shapes had been added to coffee tables and sharp corners, in the event of a head bump from Aurora. A stylish wide basket was now in the living room, filled with brightly coloured toys and a tub of interlocking building blocks.

She glanced at him, not sure what to say now they were here.

Apparently, that was mutual. Imogen sighed softly, popping Aurora down on the floor and setting her free. The two parents stood back, a couple of feet apart, watching as Aurora went off, exploring her new environment. Toddlers learned by touching, and Aurora touched *everything*—his white sofas, his glass-topped coffee table—so she was sure Luca appreciated the wisdom of having moved anything fragile out of Aurora's way. She cruised the lounge room for several minutes before discovering the basket, but when she saw it, she squealed delightedly and ran on those deliciously chubby little legs towards it, plonking herself down at the edge and half diving in to examine the contents.

She heard Luca's sharp intake of breath and slanted a look at him.

Emotion.

She saw it on his face and felt it cut through her heart.

He was looking at Aurora as though she were the most incredible, fascinating, amazing thing in the world. He was looking at her with...*love*. A lump formed in Imogen's throat, and she blinked quickly.

'Mind if I make a cup of tea?'

He glanced across at her with obvious reluctance. Like he'd forgotten she was there. Imogen's heart thumped in pain. 'Make yourself at home.'

'Would you like anything?'

'Better not ask what I would like right now.'

She closed her eyes in a wave of desperation. 'You're never going to forgive me for this, are you?' She asked the question quietly, but with an intensity that was drawn from deep in her chest.

'Would you, if our situations were reversed?'

She glanced at Aurora and felt the reality of that sink inside of her like a stone. He was right, but he was also wrong. What he was missing was the very logical place Imogen had operated from: a certainty that a baby was the last thing Luca had wanted, or would be equipped to deal with.

'Watch her a moment?' Imogen asked, and Luca stared directly at her.

'She's my daughter,' he said with palpable, raw emotion. 'Of course I'll watch her.' And he turned his back on Imogen to do exactly that.

She was so like Angelica. Heartbreakingly similar, right down to their little voices. He watched Aurora and felt the slippage of time and place, of space and self, so he was a boy again, doting on the little sister who'd surprised them all with her arrival. Angelica had loved to be tickled, to have raspberries blown on her belly. She'd worshipped Luca and followed him like a puppy, but it had never occurred to him to mind. She had been the light in all their lives.

She'd shone, like Aurora shone.

He couldn't take his eyes off his daughter, and he knew he would never let anything happen to her. This time, if he had to give his own life to save hers, he would, in a heartbeat, and heaven help anyone who got in his way.

CHAPTER FOUR

'WE SHOULD PROBABLY talk about the practicalities of this,' Imogen said tentatively, when Aurora was settled for her nap.

Luca tilted her a glance, saying nothing. He was intimidating when he was like this.

Imogen forced herself to continue. 'I work three nights a week, and I teach a couple of kids piano some afternoons. I do lessons online, but generally schedule them for when Genevieve is around to help out. I've checked and she can come here, when I'm working, to look after Aurora.'

He swore softly. 'Because you do not trust me with our daughter?'

'Correct me if I'm wrong, but you don't have any experience with kids. Wouldn't you rather have some help, at least in the beginning?'

Something in his eyes shifted, an emotion she couldn't comprehend. 'I'm a quick study.'

'I...admire your confidence.' She sat down on the edge of an armchair, pulling her hair over one shoulder. 'But this is our daughter. I can't go to work unless I know she's safe.'

His features tightened perceptibly now. 'You don't think I can protect her?'

'That's a little dramatic. I'm not talking about some big bad wolf storming through the door. I just mean in case she falls over, or makes a run for the stairs.' She gestured around the apartment. 'Toddlers are non-stop. You have to be vigilant the whole time.'

'I intend to be.'

Imogen nodded slowly.

'You don't look reassured.'

Imogen's eyes widened. 'It's just—'

'She doesn't know me,' he said, crossing his arms over his chest.

And whose fault is that?

He didn't say it, but he might as well have. Imogen's cheeks flushed pink. 'What would you have done, if I'd told you back then?'

He hadn't been expecting the question; she could tell by the way his head jerked a little. 'I don't know.'

'Would you have made me move in with you then? What would you have said?'

'What I might have done doesn't really matter, as I never got the chance. I'm more interested in what you thought I'd do. That, after all, is the reason I was denied knowing her.'

Imogen flinched, but it was a fair question. 'I thought you'd completely flip out.'

Despite the seriousness of the conversation, the smallest ghost of a smile tilted his lips for a fraction of time before the thunder-clouds took over again.

'Difficult conversations still have to be had.'

'Our last difficult conversation was kind of hard for me to get over. I wasn't in the headspace for another.'

She toyed with her fingers, standing and moving towards the side table. It still had some interesting objects atop it, because it was too high for Aurora's curious little fingers. She picked up a glossy shell, running her fingers over its crenellations.

The truth was, she'd been depressed. After that morning, she'd gone into a dark, dark place and hadn't known how she'd ever get out of it. She'd barely existed. It was Aurora who had pulled her out of that funk, slowly but surely.

'Maybe I wasn't thinking clearly,' she said with a lift of one shoulder. 'At the time, I was sure it was the best decision for everyone.'

'You claimed to love me,' he said, and she shivered, hearing that word in his mouth, remembering how badly she'd wanted him to say it back to her. How *sure* she'd been that he would, because every moment they'd shared had *felt* like love to Imogen.

How stupid she'd been!

'And yet you really thought withholding a child from me was the best decision? How could you deny a child the presence of a man you claimed to love?'

'I didn't love you.'

Imogen had fantasised about saying those words for so long, and she'd thought it would be a heady delirium to throw them at his feet if ever she got the chance, but saying them now, she just felt very hollow.

Nonetheless, she spun around to face him, still clutching the shell, and she caught the shadow of surprise on his face and was glad. 'You were right. It was just sex. I loved sleeping with you, that's all.' She sucked in a breath, wondering why she didn't feel more victorious. 'Was it any wonder? I was a virgin, of course I got swept up in the excitement of it all.' She waited for the hit to land, then moved on, her voice soft and sadly reflective. 'I did like you, though. I thought you liked me. But the way you spoke to me made me realise I didn't even know you, and I sure as hell didn't think you had the emotional maturity to be a parent.'

He flinched and silence fell. She waited, breath held, for him to respond. To say something. To fight with her, to push her to admit that she had in fact loved him. Because she had, of course. Utterly and completely. But for pride, she'd lied to him now and she was glad.

Silence stretched, static and painful.

'If it makes you feel better, and you think it's best for Aurora, your sister can come over when you work.'

Tears threatened to fill Imogen's eyes. Not because he'd conceded the point but because he'd let her assertion stand, and she wanted to correct the record now and tell him she'd loved him with all her stupid, stupid heart.

She spun away, replacing the shell before swiftly leaving the room.

He stared at the wall for a long time after she left. Stared, replayed their conversation, pulling it apart, answering her questions to himself, now that he could explore them properly.

What *would* he have done if she'd told him back then?

Married her? Been secretly thrilled because he was actually missing her in his life?

He hadn't expected to. He'd truly believed he'd get over Imogen quickly, but she was a uniquely fascinating woman and a month with her had changed his parameters. He hadn't found her easy to forget, and months later, in the time frame of her pregnancy discovery, he'd been yearning for her in a way that might have weakened his resolve.

Marriage would have been wrong for her, because she would always want more than he could offer. She wouldn't be happy with a simple marriage for the sake of a baby. She would want it to be real, and he could never give her that.

He would never let himself have that, more to the point. Not after his family. Not after his failure to save them. He was going through the motions of this life, but he wasn't really living. He didn't *want* to live.

And there he found the problem, as he hadn't fully understood it then. Imogen had made him feel so alive. She'd made him feel so *happy*, in a way he hadn't deserved. She'd made him feel as though nothing in his past mattered. She'd almost made him want to forgive and forget, but he couldn't. His tribute to his family, the family he could not save, was to exist in a kind of purgatory. Imogen had threatened that with every single part of her.

She still did, he realised with a groan, dropping his head forward and transferring his intense stare to the carpet.

'I didn't love you.'

Cristo, it had felt like she was plunging a knife right through his gut, even when he recognised the sense of what she was professing. Of course she hadn't loved him. It had been a childish infatuation, nothing more, and he'd put an end to it.

But for three years, he'd had the knowledge locked in the back of his mind that if someone like Imogen Grant could love him, he wasn't all bad. It wasn't as though he'd forgiven himself for the loss of his family, and for what he'd failed to do to save them, but in his darkest moments, the fact that Imogen had loved him had been like a little touchstone of warmth deep in his cold, black heart.

And now, even that was gone; all the light had gone out.

In the few seconds it took for Imogen to properly wake up, she had the strangest sense of discombobulation. She reached for her phone to check the time only to feel air— no bedside table where hers usually was. She sat up, looking around blearily, and with another deep, dark cry, she remembered.

She was at Luca's.

He knew about Aurora.

'I didn't love you.'

'I need to get there. Stop. Let me go.'

His voice was loud, angry, raw with emotion. She pushed the sheet off herself, half worried he'd wake Aurora, half worried about him, and ran the short distance down the corridor, from her bedroom to his. She flung open the door without hesitation.

Luca was asleep, eyes shut, body naked—from the waist up at least—and sheened in perspiration. He thrashed as she watched, hitting the mattress. 'Stop! No! I have to get there, she's crying for me!' He slipped into Italian, and she recognised a dark curse in the midst of a string of other words.

Imogen had no idea what his nightmare was about, but it was terrifying to see Luca like this. Luca who was always in control, Luca who had a cool strength inherent to him.

'Luca.' She said his name loudly, sharply, but her voice shook.

He made a sound, barely human, and when she moved to him, it was partly because she was still worried he'd wake Aurora, but mostly, it was because she couldn't bear to see him like this. She told herself she would have done the same for *anyone*. Her humanity required her to offer help and comfort when needed.

She moved quickly to his bed and put her hands on his shoulders, steadying him. His skin was warm to touch, almost feverish, and his brow was covered in a light sheen of perspiration. Pity twisted her gut.

'Luca, Luca.' She shook him.

'Let me go,' he cried, louder. But he wasn't talking to her; he was in his dream. His nightmare. She'd never seen him like this—couldn't have imagined it was possible for him to feel such pain. 'I have to go!'

'It's me. It's Imogen.'

His eyes burst open and stared at her without really seeing. His face was lined with panic, his body prone with alertness. She kept her hands on his shoulders, holding him to the mattress. Not that she was any match for him physically—she just hoped he wouldn't lash out in his dreamlike state.

'You're okay,' she said, voice husky now, reassuring him. 'You're home. Everything's okay. Everything's okay.'

He frowned, as if still not comprehending. His body was so tense, his face so unfamiliar to her. He shifted a little, frowning and her heart turned over.

Her need to comfort and reassure him, to draw him back into the present, was her guiding light. Instincts were at the helm—instincts, she kept telling herself, she would have felt if it were any other person. But that wasn't completely true. There was no one else on earth she would have attempted to soothe in the following manner. For a moment later, without forethought, she leaned down, her lips finding his on autopilot, tasting the salt of his perspiration as she kissed him, swallowing the rapid husk of his breathing, hoping to draw him back into the reality of this life, and away from whatever had been torturing his sleep.

Stop! a voice in her head commanded her, shrieking at her to remember who he was and what he'd done to her, how he'd forced her to move into his home. To remember how capable he was of wounding her. And yet he was also a man, tortured by a dream, and this was just a kiss, after all—something they'd done plenty of times in the past without it ever meaning anything.

Until the threads of Luca's nightmare frayed and broke, returning him to his usual self, and he was not responding in a state of fear, but rather something else. Something more urgent and primal, an animalistic need that ran through them both.

His hands moved to her hips, lifting her easily and bringing her over him, and then he was kissing her back, his body shifting to free the sheet that was between them.

'You had a nightmare,' she said into his mouth, as he rolled them, so she was on her back, his powerful body atop.

'Yes,' he agreed—which was more than she'd expected— and then he was kissing her so hard it was impossible to talk, much less think. She arched her back, her hunger for him catching her completely off guard. And yet why should it have? Wasn't this the way it was with them? Wasn't this their normal? No matter what she thought intellectually or knew to be true and right, this was an undeniable reality with them, and she couldn't fight it.

Not then.

Not when he needed her.

When he needed her, she would be there for him. Not because she cared about him—she wouldn't be that stupid ever again—but because he was a human being, in pain, and she was right there, and knew how to fix it.

Only it wasn't selfless.

Imogen needed fixing too.

Imogen needed the sense of wholeness and euphoria that came from being with Luca. When they were together, everything was right in the world, and she didn't need to think beyond that. How could she feel that way, after everything that had happened with them? She hated him, and yet she hated seeing him hurt. She hated him, and yet she needed him too. She needed *him* to need *her*. Proof that those awful words he'd thrown at her three long years ago had been a lie—it was something to cling to, a small power she held over him that was somehow mollifying and reassuring.

But that was almost too academic. When it came down to it, Imogen sometimes felt that being with Luca went beyond a choice: it was something that was almost predestined with the two of them, something that she could fight tooth and nail but never fully control.

Except it didn't change anything between them. Tomorrow, the sun would dawn, and they'd be in the exact same predicament, the trap created by Aurora's birth, but they would have had this—at least it was something, in the chaos of their lives, a small silver lining to this whole damned mess.

She remembered where he kept his condoms and reached across towards the bedside table, but her arms weren't long enough. Not when she was pinned beneath him on the bed.

'Please,' she groaned, lifting her hips.

He grunted his agreement, stretching out to open the drawer and remove a string of contraceptives. She didn't think about how well stocked he was. She didn't think about the fact he'd undoubtedly replaced her again and again in the three years since she'd left him.

Not now.

Not when he was sheathing himself and taking her, pushing deep inside so Imogen cried out and writhed beneath him, waves of pleasure washing over her until she couldn't think straight.

Thinking was overrated anyway.

He had sworn this wouldn't happen. Hell, he'd wanted to keep her at arm's length, but in the tumult of his nightmare, in the torture of those memories, he'd woken to see Imogen, and she'd been like a beacon, a light in the abject darkness of his grief and failings, looking at him with her sweet, kind face, with all the goodness that glowed from her like starlight.

He'd wanted to shout at her, because her kindness and concern were the last things he wanted. His nightmare had been awful; his stomach was churning, just like it had that night, and he'd been relishing that pain, because he deserved it. How long had it been since he'd had a nightmare? In the beginning, they'd been frequent, but then he'd managed to control even his dreams. It must have been seeing Aurora. She was so like Angelica, so like his little sister, the memories had been stirred up and brought to life once more. And he'd been glad! Glad to exist in that pain and torture. But then Imogen had leaned down and kissed him, and any intention to control the spark that flared between them had been lost in the sheer urgency of their coming together.

He glanced across at her sleeping face, so innocent and

beautiful, so achingly familiar, and regret slammed into him hard. Regret for his weakness, her kindness, for the passion that seemed determined to rule their interactions, even when they both clearly wished they didn't feel it.

There was nothing for it; Luca would simply have to try harder to control this. Imogen had offered herself to him once before, on a silver platter, and he'd known it to be impossible. Her love had been the last thing he'd wanted, the last thing he could accept, and nothing had changed. She wasn't offering love now, but she was still offering more than he would ever let himself have. She was still offering him a balm to his past, a way to forget, maybe even to forgive, and for that reason alone, Luca would hold firm. Imogen was not, and never could be, his, in any way.

She must have fallen asleep because it was dawn when she woke in his bed, then rolled to her side so she could look at him.

And her stomach churned because this was so familiar. Waking early, seeing his face, knowing she wouldn't have long before he stirred and started preparing for his day. Showering—always alone—dressing into one of those immaculate suits, gradually putting up all his barriers and pushing her away.

She hadn't realised it at the time, but Imogen had had three years to reflect and consider, and now she saw his morning rituals as a form of excising her from his life. Of showing her he didn't want her to be there more than she had been.

Why hadn't she understood that at the time?

She contemplated leaving his room, creeping out to

avoid having to be pushed away again, but Imogen was older and wiser now, and more determined to do things on her terms. Whatever that might mean.

As if her being awake had somehow communicated itself to him, he blinked his eyes open and they landed straight on her, so her skin fizzed with a strange awareness, and her body trembled.

She didn't say good morning, and nor did he. It was almost too banal for them, after what had happened last night.

'You had a nightmare,' she said, as she had the night before, only this time, a question was couched in her words.

His jaw tightened.

'What was it about?'

His eyes darkened. 'I don't remember.'

Imogen's heart panged as if screws were being tightened on both sides. 'Don't you?' Scepticism tinged her words.

'It was just a dream.'

'No, it was a nightmare,' she insisted, as frustration whipped at her spine. 'You must have thought I was so stupid,' she said softly, pitying her twenty-two-year-old self.

Luca's frown showed he didn't understand.

'You did that *all the time* back then and I didn't even realise.'

'Did what?'

'Deflect. Not answer. I'd ask you a question and you'd deftly sidestep it, or turn it into a question about me instead. I hardly knew you, Luca, and all the while I was an open book to you.'

A muscle jerked in his jaw, but he didn't deny it.

'You're doing it now. If you don't want to talk about your nightmare, then just say that. You don't have to lie to me. I know what I saw.'

'And what did you see?'

She frowned slowly, searching for words. 'You were terrified. No, you were haunted.' She shuddered. 'It was awful.'

He pushed back the sheet and stepped out of bed, gloriously naked and uncaring, striding towards the en suite. It was all so familiar, she felt as though she'd been sucked back in time. He'd pushed her away so often then, but she'd been living in a fantasy land, failing to recognise what he was doing. She saw it now and it hurt like hell. She hurt for this moment, but also for all the moments that had gone before. For the younger woman she'd been, who'd loved so unquestioningly, so trustingly, and had been blind to what he'd been showing her all along.

He'd been using her. Using her for sex, for pleasure, because she was easy. Just like he'd been using her last night, to forget his nightmare. Nothing with Luca was real, and nothing with Luca was ever about Imogen. This was what Luca needed, what Luca wanted.

And damn it if she didn't keep letting him do it to her. She kept throwing herself at him, no matter what happened between them. She kept making it easy for him to make love to her,

But she was different now, she reminded herself once more. She was older, wiser and refused to soften towards him. She knew what he was now, when she hadn't then. As she had promised Genevieve, she refused to let her guard down with him.

'Then you have your answer,' he said, when he reached

the door to the bathroom, surprising her, because she presumed his departure had signalled the end of their conversation. 'And yes,' he admitted, uneasily. 'It was more awful than I care to explain.'

Imogen would have said there weren't many things about Luca that could surprise her now. She knew he was callous, cold, selfish, unfeeling. But she hadn't expected *this* version of him. The Luca who was sitting opposite their daughter, lifting fingers of toast and aeroplaning them towards Aurora in a way that made the little toddler giggle with total abandon before stuffing the toast into her mouth and munching it with classic Aurora enthusiasm.

The contrast with the dark, tortured man she'd made love to the night before and *this* version of him was giving her whiplash.

'She's a good eater,' Luca said, with genuine admiration, turning to Imogen.

Her breath hitched in her throat because in that moment, he was just a dad, discovering things about his daughter, and loving it. Loving her.

Imogen's heart felt heavy and detached from her body. So, he was capable of loving after all. Just not of loving Imogen.

She nodded quickly, trying not to let that realisation hurt. 'She's adored food from the moment we introduced solids.'

'We?'

'Gen and me. Gen's been invaluable.' Luca turned back to Aurora, but not before Imogen caught the look of anger in his eyes.

'What else?' he asked, though, continuing the conversation.

'What else?' She took a seat at the table, a little way down. Observing but not intruding. Luca was right: he'd missed so much. This was his chance to make up for lost time, and Imogen had no need to get in the way.

'What else does she like, besides toast?'

'Oh, right.'

'Baba chimiken,' Aurora said, showing she didn't miss a beat.

'Butter chicken,' Imogen translated.

Luca raised a brow.

'Pasta. Rice. She's really good with vegetables. I make a broccoli soup that she can't get enough of. Cheese sticks, cucumber.' Imogen wracked her brain. 'I took her for sushi a couple of weeks ago and that was fun. Messy but fun.'

'Sushi.' He nodded slowly, as if cataloguing the list in his brain.

'She's very adventurous,' Imogen continued, because he wanted the gaps filled in and she possessed the information necessary. 'Not just with food, but with anything. She loves to go down slides—the higher the better. And to be pushed in the swings—same thing. I can never push her high enough. She loves see-saws but that makes me nervous so we don't do that too often.'

She watched as Luca took another piece of toast, flying it through the air with a buzzing engine noise. Her heart had gone way past painful and throbbed into no-longer-capable-of-beating territory. Years ago, she'd dreamed of this—of their happily-ever-after. She'd believed they were falling in love, that they would marry and have children, a family of their own. Those dreams were childish, not based in reality. She'd accepted that. So living, now, in a version of those dreams—one that was lined with darkness and enmity—was almost impossible to bear.

'Does she go to nursery?'

Imogen shook her head, trying to dislodge her painful thoughts. 'She's too young. She's made friends with some kids who go, though. She watches them scooter off in the mornings and can't wait to join them.' Imogen swallowed quickly. 'Sometimes I feel like she's the most independent toddler that's ever existed.'

'Independence is not a bad thing.'

'No, it's not. But it can be hard,' Imogen admitted with a wistful smile.

'Hard how?'

'I don't know. I guess I can already imagine the day she packs up and moves out.'

Luca turned to Imogen, scanning her face thoughtfully. 'There are worse things to imagine.'

Imogen frowned at the cryptic remark. He was right, but that didn't invalidate her feelings.

'It's just all going so fast. I feel like she was a new-born three seconds ago, and now look at her.'

Aurora finished the last piece of toast then started to pull at the restraint of her high chair.

'Breakfast is over,' Imogen said with a smile, as Luca went to clear Aurora's plate.

'I'll do that,' Imogen murmured. 'Why don't you play with her?' And then she added, 'I'll be in the kitchen, if you need me.'

Need her?

Of course he didn't need her.

Not only was Luca Romano apparently a Wunderkind in the business world, when it came to looking after their daughter, he had the skills of Mary Poppins. Of course.

Because he was just frustratingly good at everything. Except peopling, she reminded herself.

She should have been glad that he was adapting so well to the role of fatherhood, but she wasn't, because every time she saw him with Aurora, she was hit right in between her eyes with doubt as to her decision to keep them apart. It had seemed so obvious at the time, she hadn't once questioned her choice. But now?

How could she not?

She kept busy in the kitchen. Hiding, she admitted to herself. Initially, she cleaned up the breakfast dishes but then, she made a brownie with the ingredients she found in Luca's walk-in pantry, before cleaning up those dishes, so when he strode in almost two hours after breakfast was finished, the air was heavy with the smell of sweets.

'There have been four yawns in the last ten minutes. I take it it's nap time?' he prompted, looking at Aurora, who was snuggled into his hip.

'Yeah,' Imogen said, her voice throaty, her eyes suspiciously stinging. Aurora just looked so *right* on Luca's hip. She was so comfortable with him already. They were father and daughter, and Aurora seemed to somehow just understand that.

Imogen spun away quickly, busying herself with washing her hands and making a meal of it to buy for time.

'I'll take her up,' she said, when she could trust herself to speak.

But Luca waved her away. 'I can do it. At least, I think I can.'

'I have to change her diaper.' Imogen shook her head.

'I can do that too.'

'Really? Have you had much practice with changing a toddler's diaper?'

'More than you know,' he said, before turning on his heel and leaving.

What? What toddler? she wanted to call after him, but with Aurora on his hip, it wasn't the time to interrogate him, and so she stayed downstairs, one ear trained for calls for help while she set about making some sandwiches for their lunch. She wasn't really hungry, but it was something to do with her hands, something to help distract her, and God knew she needed that.

He was surprised by how much of caring for Aurora was, in fact, muscle memory. From feeding her to carrying her to placing her down for her nap, it all brought back so many memories of Angelica. And more than his little sister, it brought back memories of his late mother's voice, as she'd gently instructed him on the way to hold a baby, then a toddler; on the best methods for settling a little one into bed.

He knew he didn't need to stay with Aurora as she fell asleep, but he did so anyway, driven to watch her drift off for very selfish reasons. Firstly, he had missed so much of his daughter's life that he was now gripped by a visceral need to absorb absolutely everything. To watch as her lashes fluttered over her velvet-soft cheeks and her breathing grew slumberous.

But he was also avoiding Imogen.

Avoiding her intense stare, her perceptive eyes, her always kind questions. Avoiding her because she confused him, and made him forget everything he had sworn to himself.

Avoiding her because when he was with her, he wanted her.

She helped him forget, yes, but she also made him feel

something other than this heart-rending grief and guilt, the gift that Imogen had always bestowed upon him. A gift he had no place accepting, let alone craving.

Imogen was off-limits. She should have been so three years ago, and she sure as hell was now—he just had to remember that.

CHAPTER FIVE

'LUCA, WHAT DID you mean before?'

She asked the question as soon as he returned to the kitchen, sometime after leaving to settle Aurora for her nap. And she asked the question with the full expectation that he would deflect, as always. Frustration champed at the edges of her belly; she braced for his defensive technique, but still she waited in silence.

'When?'

Sure enough, there was a cautious caginess to his voice, as though he knew she was buying time to work out his best obfuscation technique.

'When you said you had more experience with toddlers than I realised.'

His eyes met hers, carefully blanked of expression. Yet his jaw clenched visibly, and she felt his reluctance. 'It means you can count on me.'

'No,' she persisted, once again marvelling at how stupid she'd been three years earlier to have let him put her off so easily. 'That's not what I'm asking.'

'I know what you're asking.' He jammed his hands into his pockets, his jaw set in a mutinous line.

'So?' she prompted, refusing to let this go.

'What do you want me to say?'

'It's a simple question.' She stood firm. 'You made a statement. I'm asking what it meant.'

He opened his mouth to speak, then closed it, looking away sharply before removing one hand from his pocket and dragging a hand over his stubbled jaw. 'Aurora isn't the first toddler I've spent time with.' His voice was clipped, as if each word was resented.

He didn't want to talk about this, but Imogen wasn't prepared to let it go—not until she understood. Luca had indeed been a closed book to her, but that was no longer an acceptable proposition to Imogen. 'Who else?'

His eyes flicked to hers, then away again. 'That's not important.'

She sighed heavily. He wanted to keep hold of this particular barrier, hard and impenetrable. He wanted to make it impossible for her to understand him. Why? What was he hiding? And why had he referred to his experience with kids in the first place, then? Or had his admission simply slipped out?

'You can't have it both ways, Luca. If you don't want to talk about something, don't drop cryptic little hints.'

His brows shot up, his face angling back to hers. 'That wasn't my intention.'

She rolled her eyes, frustrated beyond belief with the man. Frustrated with how their relationship had been then, and how it was now. 'Fine,' she grunted with a hint of anger. 'Have it your way.' She pushed away from the bench and began to stalk towards the kitchen door, but right before she reached it, his hand snaked out and curled around her wrist, arresting her, so she turned to face him, scanning his features. His grip wasn't hard. The touch, if anything, was gentle, but every cell in her body sprung to life in response, which seemed to sear her skin.

'I had a little sister.' His voice was cool, his eyes locked to hers but revealing nothing. His features were bland. It was as if he were speaking from a part of him to which he had no access, reciting lines by rote, refusing to allow himself to feel them. 'She died when she was two and a half.'

Imogen reached behind her, needing to hold something for support.

'Her name was Angelica.' He paused, the silence heavy with Luca's pained confession and Imogen's questions. 'Aurora looks just like her.'

Imogen stared at him, utterly and totally shocked into silence for several long beats.

'I had— I didn't— You never mentioned her. I had no idea.'

'I know that.'

'Why didn't you tell me?'

'Why would I?'

'We were dating for a month, Luca. It seems like something that would have come up.'

'We weren't dating.' The words were almost a curse in his mouth. She pulled away from him, stepping back, her temper and hurt in conflict with her empathy.

'What happened to her?' she whispered, desperately sad to think of anything happening to a dear little toddler.

'That's not—something I care to discuss. She died. It was sudden.'

'Your nightmare,' Imogen murmured, and now empathy won out, for she stepped back towards him, putting her hands on his cheeks, holding his face. 'You were dreaming about her.'

Despite her grasp, he angled his face away, glaring at the window as if he were about to punch it.

'You asked about my experience with children and I told you. I don't want to discuss it any further.'

She dropped her hands to her sides, suppressing a sigh. She had to respect his choice. More than that, she supposed she should have been somewhat grateful that he'd confided in her, even to some small degree. She could see how hard it had been for him.

'How old were you, when she died?'

His Adam's apple shifted as he swallowed. 'It was the night of my twelfth birthday.'

Imogen closed her eyes on a wave of comprehension. The night they'd met had been his thirtieth birthday; he'd been in a terrible mood, determined to get blind drunk until they'd met and his plans had taken a detour. Then the other night had been his thirty-third birthday, and he'd come to the same bar, for the same purpose.

She bit into her lip. Despite the way he'd treated her, and how angry she was with him, she couldn't help but feel sorry for him too.

'That must have been so hard, Luca.'

He visibly clenched his teeth. 'I didn't tell you for sympathy. I told you to explain. I know what I'm doing with our daughter—to some extent.'

Imogen had so many questions she wanted to ask, like what had his sister been like and how much did he do with the baby, and did he have a photograph of her? But she could see he'd stepped out of his comfort zone and was already withdrawing from Imogen, pushing her away, boxing himself into a lonely little corner.

And she couldn't care. She couldn't.

For all that she might feel sorry for him, it didn't change the fact that he had broken her heart three years ago. He had spoken to her in a way that had been designed to wound; he had discarded her as if she were nobody. He had half destroyed her, and if it hadn't been for her music, and then her pregnancy, she had no idea how she would have got through it.

'Okay.' Her voice was a little unsteady. She stepped back from him quickly. 'Well, I'm here if you need help. With Aurora,' she added, stepping further away. She disappeared into the bathroom, needing space, and the freedom to let her tears roll without Luca seeing them.

It wasn't a big deal.

It wasn't like he could have kept it from her for ever.

Like it or not, Imogen had become someone who would be in his life for good. She was Aurora's mother; he was Aurora's father. They had to work together in some capacity, and it was only natural that she should know about his life. Some of it.

When he was comfortable enough to discuss it.

It didn't mean anything that she now knew. It wasn't like it changed anything between them, nor with his guilt and grief. That was the point. There was no going back. No do-overs.

He hadn't been able to save his family and they'd all died. That was the defining moment in his life. At twelve, he'd learned what it was like to betray everyone you loved, and he'd never forgive himself for it.

Imogen didn't need to know nor understand that, but as to the facts, who cared? His family had died in a house fire on the night of his twelfth birthday. It wasn't something he could hide from her now. Not for ever. Apart from anything, Aurora would have questions, one day. Was he going to lie to her about it?

He ignored the stitching pain in his chest, the awful, awful feeling he experienced whenever he thought of his parents. Not his guilt at how they'd died, but his world-shattering pain when he remembered their lives. How great they'd been. How much he'd loved them. How strong and powerful and capable of anything they'd made him feel. How his life had been great and perfect, until it wasn't.

He boxed those feelings away, tightened his tie then strode out of the kitchen, needing space from this new domestic situation. And needing space from Imogen's intelligent, sympathetic eyes in particular.

'I'm heading to work.'

Imogen, dressed in a pair of jeans and a loose sweater, barely glanced up from the notebook she was writing in. 'Yeah, okay.' Her eyes had a dreamy, far-away look, so he wondered if she even saw him, much less heard him.

'Earth to Imogen.' He waved a hand in front of her face.

She frowned. 'I heard you.' She pulled the notebook closer without appearing to see him still. 'Have fun.'

He frowned, stalking away from her towards the back door, easing himself out of it and climbing into his car. What was she working on? What was she doing?

A frown etched itself across his face as he drove towards the City. Three years ago, she'd been like an open book, just as she'd said, talking freely about whatever he'd asked. And he *had* asked. Mainly to deflect her interest in him, just as she'd accused him of doing. But that didn't mean he hadn't enjoyed hearing her talk about herself. Her life. Her family. Her passion for music. He'd never met anyone quite like her—such a free spirit, but so dedicated to one area as well. It hadn't been about financial success for Imogen, but rather a drive to create music.

What was she doing now, besides playing in the bar and teaching kids to play piano? He pulled a face. It seemed like a waste of her talent.

Then again, it wasn't his place to get involved. They were co-parents, nothing more. Her life was none of his business; he couldn't allow himself to forget that.

Imogen and Aurora ate alone that night and Imogen tried not to think about Luca. She tried not to wonder where he was, nor to contemplate who he was with.

'I will replace you.'

She tried not to imagine his life outside the house, tried not to imagine the world she'd interrupted, albeit unwittingly. And unwillingly, come to think of it. She tried not to think about how many women he'd slept with since her, while she'd been busy raising Aurora.

But as the minutes ticked by and she went about the business of settling Aurora to bed, her temper built in waves, and she found it almost impossible to keep at bay.

She settled their daughter to sleep for the night, carefully disguising any hint of her irritation, and then went into the kitchen to make a cup of tea. The kettle had just boiled when she heard the back door close.

Her temper sparked.

She tried to tamp it down, without success. She knew it wasn't just about tonight. His being gone brought back too many memories. Too much of that same sense of frustration, at how hidden he was from her, at how he called all the shots. When he wanted Imogen, she'd been there. She'd never stopped to wonder if the same would be true in reverse.

'Why exactly did you insist on us moving in here?' she asked, whirling around to face him. Luca's face was without emotion, his eyes landing on her and giving nothing away.

'Excuse me?'

'It's eight o'clock. I've spent the last hour and a half feeding, bathing and putting Aurora to bed, and you were what? Where?'

'I told you I was going to work.'

She rolled her eyes. 'Whatever. I don't care. Just let me know in future so I can make plans.'

'What is going on here?' he demanded, crossing his arms. 'You know I work late.'

'No, I know you *used to* work late, but you've just discovered you're a father and your daughter is here. I would have thought you'd make that a priority, at least for a while. God, this is so stupid. I have been *so* stupid, yet again, to move in here with you and actually think you were capable of putting someone else first.'

His nostrils flared. 'You have been doing this on your own for more than two years. Are you telling me you couldn't cope without me?'

'No, I'm saying—' She floundered, because this wasn't really about Aurora, but rather the images she'd been conjuring all night of him making love to some other woman in some fancy hotel room or some gorgeous luxe penthouse. Some supermodel, or actress, or heiress. 'Don't worry. It doesn't matter,' she responded, her voice clipped. Their past was a visage from which she couldn't escape. Three years of imagining him moving on from her swirled like shark-infested waters all around Imogen.

She went to walk past him, cup of tea forgotten, but he caught her wrist and held her still.

'You're jealous.'

Her eyes flew to his. Anger was a dark, suffocating torrent, rising inside of her. She couldn't be jealous—at least she couldn't admit it—because it was so far outside of what she'd promised to herself, and Genevieve, when she'd come to live with Luca. She was hurt; there was a difference.

'Go to hell.'

'You think I was with another woman.'

Damn him for being able to see through her so easily. 'I don't care,' she responded quickly, coldly, but her heart was burning up and her body was trembling. 'It's none of my business.'

'Be that as it may,' he conceded with a nod, 'you are jealous.'

She looked away from him, angry because he was *right*.

Danger sirens blared. She wasn't doing a good job of keeping him at arm's length. She wasn't doing a good job with any of this.

'What do you want me to say, Imogen? Do you want me to say that I was alone in my office? Do you need to hear me say I was not with someone else? Why is that?'

She sucked in a breath, furious with him and with herself. 'I don't care who you're screwing,' she muttered.

'Liar.'

'But I don't intend to be someone you use to keep your bed warm on a quiet night. Keep your hands off me.'

And she pulled away from him with at least some sense of pride restored, stalking away from him with a spine that was ramrod straight.

He caught up to her little more than a few paces away

but he didn't touch her. 'Need I remind you, you came into *my* room and kissed me...'

'Oh, just—just—go to hell!'

His brows launched towards his hairline. 'Were you always this dramatic?'

She spun around, fire in her eyes. 'I doubt it.'

'I am not using you to keep my bed warm. This is an evolving situation, and I am as unsure about it as you are. Clearly sleeping together is a terrible idea, given what happened last time. I would like to say it wouldn't happen again. I would like to *think* I was capable of behaving with a modicum of restraint, but the thing is...' His words trailed off, and he shook his head. 'I can't make that promise, and I don't think you can either.'

She shivered, because he was being so honest, and he was right. He was fighting the same battle she was, trying not to give in to temptation, when it was like a drug...

'Why would you jump to the conclusion that I'd gone off to sleep with some other woman?'

She stared up at him, her expression mutinous. 'Because I'm replaceable, remember?' She spat the words at him, the taste of them in her mouth like acid. 'I've never forgotten, and thank God for that. It's probably the only thing stopping me from being a total fool again this time around. I'm replaceable, and you can replace me whenever you want. But please have the courtesy to give me a heads up when it happens, so I don't make dinner for you.' She tilted her chin and stalked away; this time, he didn't follow.

Once he started to remember that morning, he couldn't stop. He sat with a glass of red wine, staring at a blank wall, and heard himself. *Really* heard himself. The things he'd said to her, cold and assured, the way her face had crumpled and then dropped into her hands, so he didn't have to look at her as he berated her with all the reasons she'd been imagining anything between them.

He'd been *so* angry with her for falling in love with him. So angry with her, but he'd been even angrier with himself for being so careless. For telling himself that it was fine, that they were obviously just sleeping together and that surely she understood it meant nothing. He'd said things along the way in an attempt to convey that, to keep it light. But damn it, Imogen was too full of sunshine and warmth, too willing to see the best in anyone and everyone and she'd fallen hard for the wrong guy.

He'd told himself he'd been doing her a favour by ending it as harshly as possible, so she could forget about him and move on. But the way she'd thrown the word *replaceable* at him that night showed him how deeply he'd cut her.

He took a drink, a familiar feeling twisting low in his gut.

Guilt.

Guilt at having hurt her like that. Guilt at having led her on in the first place, just because he liked being with her. Guilt at taking the break-up too far, rather than letting her down gently. He'd panicked and he'd just needed her to go, because being loved by anyone had seemed like a total rejection of the state he deserved to live in for the rest of his life. Unknowingly, she'd stepped right over one of his most fundamental lines, a boundary he'd established as a twelve-year-old and never intended to allow to be eroded.

He hadn't wanted to hurt her, though.

He'd spent three years confident that she'd have moved on, and easily. But what if she hadn't? What if he'd cut her too deeply for that?

He dropped his head forward, the thought one he didn't even dare contemplate.

'I hate you.'

She'd said that to him that night at the bar, and he'd been glad. He was still glad. He just needed for her not to forget it.

It didn't matter that it was late. When the soft knock sounded at her door, Imogen was still wide awake, reading a book without paying any attention to the words.

'Yes?'

He pushed the door in, his features strained. 'We need to talk.'

She didn't want to talk. She wanted to do something far more physical; she just couldn't decide if it involved punching him in the gut or dragging him to her.

'Do we?' she muttered, closing the book and placing it beside her.

He strode to the edge of her bed but stayed standing. Out of reach. Probably best, for both of them.

'Three years ago, you fell in love with a fantasy of your own creation. You saw something that wasn't there. It's not your fault. Like I said—far less gently than I should have—at the time, you were young and inexperienced, and the physical nature of our relationship overwhelmed you. I should have done a better job of making sure you understood what I wanted.'

Imogen was frozen still. This conversation was her worst nightmare. She had relived the past, replayed that awful morning, enough times in her mind. She didn't want to do it again now. Not with the instrument of all that pain right in front of her.

'I told you,' she said a little unevenly. 'I wasn't in love with you. I get that now.'

'Great,' he responded, a little tightly. 'But that's not my point.'

'Well, what is then?'

'I don't want history to repeat itself.'

'Believe me, I'm not going to fall in love with you. Or think I've fallen in love with you. Never gonna happen, buddy.'

'Because the sex is still overwhelming,' he admitted gruffly, 'it's easy to confuse that with something else, but I feel the same way I did then. I am not interested in a relationship.'

Her cheeks flushed with heat.

'We're parents. And I want us to live together, at least until we find out how to do this properly. But living together is bound to lead to sleeping together and I just need to know that I've been honest with you. Honest like I should have been back then.'

She shook her head, frustration making her lips pinch. 'You seriously think I'd be stupid enough to fall for you?'

'Probably not,' he responded with a tight smile. 'I'm just trying to avoid what happened last time.'

'Last time,' she hissed, 'I had no idea what you were like. Now I do, and believe me when I tell you I'm not interested.'

He lifted one thick, dark brow.

'Okay, sex has the potential to be a complication. We just…can't let it.'

'No?' He moved closer and even just that single action, his body brushing the edge of the bed, made her skin lift in goose bumps.

'No,' she said, but her voice was hoarse. 'We're stronger than this.'

He nodded once, his eyes heavy on hers. 'I hope you are right, Imogen. There's too much at stake now for us to mess this up.'

CHAPTER SIX

THREE YEARS AGO, he'd kept her at a distance using his work as an excuse. Now it was by mutual understanding, and a healthy sense of self-preservation. Imogen didn't try to get close to him. Not like she had then. She didn't try because she didn't want to.

Three years ago, he'd smashed her heart into oblivion, and it didn't matter how great he was with Aurora—he was still that same cruel-hearted man. He was still someone who was capable of blowing hot and cold, of making her feel things that seemed so much like love, and then coldly dismissing her from his life.

She would never trust him again, and without trust, there could be no true relationship. They were parents, and somehow, despite their past, they'd found a way to interact that was respectful and courteous. But neither pushed the other for personal information. Neither tried to have deep and meaningful conversations.

They were like strangers in many ways, despite the intimacy they'd once shared.

On Imogen's first night back in the bar, she felt a churning of butterflies in her belly.

She and Luca had formed a sort of arrangement that worked for them, but having Genevieve in the house was like the cracking open of the past, a reminder of her wounds, and Imogen didn't particularly want to think about that.

Gen could not have made her own feelings about Luca more apparent.

'Genevieve, welcome,' he'd said.

'Thanks,' she'd responded, as though she'd have preferred to be just about anywhere else.

Imogen grimaced, but she didn't have a chance to speak to Genevieve before leaving. She squeezed her hand though, leaned in for a kiss and whispered, 'Be nice. For Aurora's sake.'

Genevieve rolled her eyes in response.

Luca had organised for his driver to take her to the bar—it made a nice change from public transport—and she nestled back in the comfort of the four-wheel drive, watching London pass by in a streak of lights and autumnal beauty.

The bar was packed, and she lost herself to the music of her set, singing some of her own songs, some covers, playing whatever she wanted, aware that the crowd was in the palm of her hand and loving the feeling.

She wanted to do this for a living. To make music, to sing it, to offer it to the world as her contribution to the creative landscape. It had been her calling for longer than she could remember.

But there was also Aurora, and until she'd been born, Imogen hadn't realised that being a mother could also be a passion. She loved being with her daughter. She loved having the flexibility to spend time with her, to play with her, to teach her to play piano. And with Luca in the picture, she had even more flexibility to pursue both. If he wanted to be an engaged father, she could rely on him for so much more than she ever could Genevieve. While her sister had been an amazing support, Imogen had often felt bad for leaning on her so much, even though Gen had insisted she didn't mind.

Luca was Aurora's father and if he was willing to play that role, to help take care of her, then Imogen would conceivably have more freedom to pursue her career. All the dreams she'd put on hold when she'd discovered she was pregnant were suddenly viable again.

She finished her set, took a bow, waved at the crowd then made her way off stage, towards the bar.

'Great set, Im. What'll it be?'

She couldn't say why she was delaying going back to Luca's, only that it was the first time she'd been out of the place in a week, and with it came a sense of relief. She was glad to be away from him, glad to prove to herself that she could stay away. Because everything was so complicated, and she needed to make sure she didn't lose herself again. No matter what she said to him, she wasn't an idiot. She knew there was risk here.

She knew there *could* be risk, anyway, unless she was very, very careful. She could be with him. She could spend time with him, she just couldn't ever forgive him.

If she didn't forgive him, she wouldn't fall for him again.

'Glass of white.'

'Pinot Gris?'

'Perfect.'

She watched as Leon, who was always behind the bar, poured the drink and slid it across to her. 'No charge, superstar.'

She frowned. 'That's not fair.'

'No way. The nights you play are always our busiest. I owe you.'

'You pay me to play,' she reminded him.

'Nowhere near enough.' He winked, then moved off to serve someone else.

She sat at the bar, listening to the next act, forcing herself to stay right where she was. There was no better way to prove to herself, and Luca, that she was totally her own woman than by staying out just a little later and enjoying another musician. Even when her nerves were stretching taut, and she was itching to get back to his place.

She finished the glass and stood up, weaving through the crowd and out the side door, where Luca's car was waiting, the driver reading a book behind the wheel. She tapped lightly on the window, clearly startling him, for which she apologised.

He moved quickly but she waved him away. 'I can open my own door,' she said with a smile.

'All part of the service,' he quipped, opening it for her regardless.

She slipped in and sighed, pleased that she'd passed this milestone, pleased that she was being mature enough to make this work. Pleased all round, that what had seemed like a disaster a week ago wasn't actually turning out to be so bad.

'Your sister hates me too.'

'Too?'

'In addition to you, remember?' he reminded her, when she walked back into the room, having farewelled Genevieve—who did indeed despise Luca, more than words could say.

'Oh, right.' She lifted one shoulder. 'She's protective of me.'

His eyes lingered on Imogen's face a moment, long enough for her heart to thump and her skin to prickle with goose bumps, then walked towards an armchair and took a seat opposite.

'How was it?'

She smiled. 'Great.'

His eyes roamed her face. 'You're an excellent performer.'

Heat flushed her cheeks. 'I love it.'

'How many nights do you play at the bar?'

'Just three per week at the moment.'

'And you teach piano, you said?'

She nodded.

'Is that what you aspired to, Imogen?'

Her eyes widened.

'This. Your work. Is it what you dreamed of?'

'To make a living from music? Absolutely.'

He frowned though, a quick quirk of his lips.

'You don't approve?'

'It's not my place to approve or not.'

'Nonetheless, you're clearly thinking something. What?'

'I seem to remember you wanting to move to America, to get a recording deal with one of the big labels.'

Her heart thudded against her ribs. He remembered that?

Of course he remembered. He was smart and switched on, and she'd opened her soul to him, including her professional aspirations.

'I got pregnant,' she reminded him. Then, realising that might sound like a criticism, she softened her tone a little. 'And it was a blessing. It didn't feel like it at the time, but Aurora turned everything around for me. I still have aspirations, but they're not the only thing I focus on now. Maybe when she's older,' Imogen said with a lift of one shoulder.

His frown deepened. 'I didn't know about her,' he said, needlessly. Imogen was well aware of the facts. They'd discussed them ad nauseam, after all. 'I wasn't there to help you, but I am now.'

Imogen's eyes widened. It was exactly what she'd been thinking in the bar. Everything was different now that Luca was in the picture. Seeing how great he was with Aurora had opened up a door for her she'd been reluctant to look for earlier. While Genevieve was an amazing help, Imogen was reluctant to impose too much. With Luca, she didn't have the same concerns. Aurora was his child, and he'd made it abundantly clear he wanted to help.

'There is kind of an opportunity,' she said, her lips pulling to the side. 'A label that's interested in me. They want me to submit a demo.' She waved a hand through the air, tamping down on the instant rush of excitement, keeping her feet firmly planted in reality. 'It's not a big deal. It probably won't come to anything, but it's an opportunity at least. It would mean a bit of time in a studio. A few days, probably...'

He didn't smile. He didn't congratulate her. But he leaned forward, his elbows on his thighs, and said, 'I have a recording studio you could use.'

Her heart kerthunked. 'You do?'

'Sure.'

'Um, where?'

'It's at my place in Tuscany—I bought the villa from a

musician—the recording studio is state of the art, though obviously I've never used it.'

'You have a place in Tuscany?'

'Does that surprise you? I'm Italian.'

'But you live here.'

'My businesses are headquartered here. My home is in Italy.'

She stared at him, surprised by that. Surprised that it had never occurred to her. Surprised, most of all, by his willingness to help her. Then again, it was easy for him to do. He had a home with a recording studio, and the means to travel the world at the drop of a hat. Still, she couldn't help but feel a flood of warmth at how quickly he'd extended his support to her. Like he cared about her life, and her career.

'Let me do this for you,' he said, intensely, as though mistaking her silence for hesitation. 'I owe you this.'

'You owe me?'

'Who knows what your life would be like if I'd been a part of Aurora's from birth?'

She shook her head, dispelling that sentiment. 'I didn't tell you about her, remember?'

'I remember,' he replied, but without the sting of their prior arguments on the matter. This was almost conversational. 'I do not believe our daughter should ever be a reason that you have not succeeded in your career.'

She shook her head. 'I don't see it that way. I love what I do—'

'You have a gift.' His words slammed into her. They were emphatic and insistent, as though he *needed* her to see it his way. 'You should share it with as many people as you are able. Of course you should record a demo, and the recording label would be stupid not to snap you up.'

His blind faith in her almost brought tears to her eyes. She hadn't expected such passionate support from Luca, of all people.

'For years, your voice has been in my mind,' he muttered. And now, a hint of his resentment was back, a rush of darkness that he hadn't been strong enough to blot her from his memory. 'Your songs, your sound, the way you can sing as though yours is the only voice to ever find a melody. It is…mesmerising.'

'Mesmerising,' she whispered, thinking that, if anything, it was *his* words that were addictive, his voice that had cycled around and around in her mind until she'd almost lost touch with reality.

'Addictive,' he added, his eyes boring into hers, like he was as bound by the power of this stare as Imogen was. She couldn't look away; she was powerless in the face of his offer, and his admission. 'I woke up hearing you.'

The hairs on the back of her neck stood on end.

'Come to Italy with me, Imogen,' he implored again, throatily, raw, and her heart palpitated against her ribs.

How could she say no? Setting aside the fact he was taking away any practical barrier to her recording this album, there was something else tightening inside her chest, making her yearn to agree with him. If Imogen were honest with herself, she'd admit that it wasn't just about recording the demo.

Here was Luca, a man who had fiercely guarded every aspect of his private life from her, even as they'd been as intimate as any two people could ever be, offering her a glimpse behind the curtain. His home in Italy must mean something to him, as it was where he was from.

Something like hope surged inside Imogen, but she

tamped it down, just as she did when she thought of her music.

'Aurora…' she said thoughtfully.

'Will come with us, naturally,' he interrupted, misunderstanding.

Imogen swallowed. 'She doesn't have a passport.'

'Leave that to me,' he said with easy authority.

Imogen bit down on her lip. 'Luca—'

'We can go to Italy as soon as that's organised.'

Imogen toyed with her fingers, nervous suddenly. But there was nothing for it; he'd find out for himself soon enough. 'There's something you should know about Aurora.'

He waited with the appearance of patience.

'She has my last name. You're not… I couldn't put you on her birth certificate.'

His eyes briefly closed. She could feel the tension emanating from him. 'Okay,' he said after a moment, and there was no sign of anger in his tone. 'We can fix that.'

Fix it.

Because she'd messed up. It hadn't felt like it at the time, and she couldn't have put his name down, anyway, without having Luca there. She'd made her peace with that situation, but having seen the two of them together now, she felt that lapse deep in her heart. 'You have a high profile. I thought…'

'You wanted to hide her from me.' The words lacked emotion, but Imogen had an abundance of them.

'I—didn't want you to be blindsided.'

'How did that work out?' he responded, then shook his head, as if to dismiss the subject. 'You made a decision. We've dealt with that.'

She nodded slowly, knotting her fingers together, glad

he was apparently so accepting of that, finally. 'Do you have any other homes, Luca?'

'*Sì.*'

Her lips twisted into a smile without her consent. She'd always loved it when he slipped into Italian. Usually it was in bed, in the heat of passion, when a string of foreign words would curl around her, warm and delicious.

'Where?' She settled back into the sofa, strangely relaxed now.

'New York, Paris, Sydney, Singapore.'

'So, just the usual then?'

His grin surprised her. It warmed her. She tamped down on the feeling, sat up straighter, let the feeling of relaxation go, to be replaced by wariness. She couldn't do this again. She wouldn't let herself soften towards him, to see things that weren't there. Wishful thinking had no place in their relationship; Luca was being kind to her, but that didn't mean he was a changed man. As far as she was concerned, the man opposite her, who was now bending over backwards to help her career, was the same bastard who'd broken her heart, utterly and completely, three years earlier.

'Anyway, I'm beat,' she lied, standing then, brushing her hands over the front of her jeans. She needed a break from the emotional juggernaut that was careening her from one emotion to the next, but mostly, she needed to escape the temptation of spending any more time with this man she'd once loved… 'I'll see you in the morning.'

She slipped away, her heart pounding, trying not to think how good it had felt to just sit and talk with Luca. That was most certainly not a safe path to travel.

* * *

She knew he was wealthy. Obviously. His house in London was huge and in one of the most exclusive areas, he had a fancy car and a full-time driver, he wore suits that were made for his frame—hand stitched and clearly expensive—and there was an air about him that spoke of money and luxury. But it wasn't until the trip to Tuscany that she really comprehended the sheer scale of his wealth.

They boarded his private jet at City Airport. It was as big as a commercial plane, shiny white with a jet-black tail and a bold white 'R' there, denoting it as his. Inside was like the lobby of a five-star hotel. Elegant armchairs, coffee tables, lamps. Walls partitioning the front section of the plane from the middle, which boasted two bedrooms, either side of the aisle. Beyond that, there were bathrooms, but unlike the usual airline offerings, these had proper showers, space to get changed, lovely lighting and décor. Right in the back there were seats more akin to a commercial airline's business class seating section—wide and with full recline abilities.

'For staff,' he said. 'Or if I need to convey multiple guests.'

'Do you do that often?'

'I use the plane for business,' he said with a lift of his shoulders. 'Meetings around the world. That involves taking members of my team with me sometimes.'

Imogen settled Aurora on one of the plush seats and buckled her in. 'You know, I have no idea what you do, Luca.'

'I invest.'

She glanced at him, scanning his face. 'What does that mean?'

'Putting money behind something I believe in.'

Imogen rolled her eyes. 'I know what it means, as a dictionary definition. I mean, what do you personally invest in?'

'A number of things. Property, commercial interests, the tech sector.'

She sat beside Aurora and clipped her seat belt together. Luca took the seat opposite them, his long legs permanently at risk of invading Imogen's space, of brushing against her own legs, if he wasn't careful. Aurora made a gabbling noise, and tried to reach for the lamp. Imogen distractedly reached into her handbag, pulled out an old, much-favoured picture book and passed it to the little girl.

'Do you enjoy it?'

He looked at her as though she'd asked if he spoke Martian. 'It's what I do. I'm good at it.'

It was Imogen's turn to look confused. 'Is it what you wanted to do as a kid?'

His eyes darkened momentarily and he glanced towards the window. It was a lovely autumnal day, clear blue skies, crisp and cool. 'I don't remember.'

Liar.

'We're ready for take-off, sir.' A pretty woman in her twenties clipped efficiently into the cabin. She wore a business suit, and her bright blond hair was secured into a fiercely tight bun. Imogen's stomach popped with unwelcome jealousy.

'I will replace you.'

She flipped the page on Aurora's book, pointing at a picture of a witch with big warts on her nose and enormous pink shoes. Aurora laughed, as she always did, at the absurdity of the image.

'Would you care for any refreshments?' The woman glanced from Imogen to Luca, her cherry-red lips curving into a full smile when she glanced at him.

'Imogen?' He looked at her though, and her stomach popped for a different reason.

She bit into her lip, shook her head once.

'Some champagne,' he said. 'And strawberries for Aurora.'

Imogen's heart turned over. She pointed at another picture and pulled a face that made Aurora giggle once more, then turned the page again. Aurora said the words that were on the page, not because she could read them but because she'd been read the book so many times it was rote for her now.

When Imogen glanced at Luca, he was staring at them with an intensity that made her pulse go haywire.

'Do you just travel with a buffet of fruit on board?' she asked, simply for something to say.

'There's a selection, yes.'

Imogen glanced around. 'This plane is incredible.'

The crew member returned with a glass of champagne, a coffee and some strawberries.

'You're not having one?' Imogen asked, curling her feet up beneath her on the plush armchair.

'You seemed nervous.'

She tried not to care that he'd noticed. 'I'm…overawed, I guess. This is incredibly opulent.'

'You get used to it.'

She shook her head, marvelling at the sheer volume of things she didn't know about Luca. 'Did you grow up like this?' she asked, gesturing around the plane.

'No.'

Imogen tried not to be shocked by the fact he'd actually answered her question instead of hedging around it. When they'd first started dating—or, rather, sleeping together—she'd searched his name on the internet and found a heap of dry biographical information to do with his company, but even that hadn't really told her what he did on a day-to-day basis. It was all corporate speak and for Imogen, who existed in a musician's bubble most of the time, it had just bored her. But there'd been nothing more personal about Luca anywhere, and she'd looked. Oh, there'd been some photos of him at events— fundraising dinners and the like—and yes, she'd noticed that he was always with a beautiful woman. Back then, she'd felt a hint of pique that he hadn't invited her to any of those events, but because she'd had her rose-coloured glasses on, she'd invented a narrative that it was because he didn't want to share her.

What a fool she'd been.

'Your parents aren't wealthy like this?'

A slight pause. 'No.'

'So you just invested your way to this lifestyle?'

'*Sì.*' The engines began to whirl, and the plane pushed back from the hangar. Aurora looked around, slightly alarmed, but with a reassuring smile from Imogen, she relaxed.

'You'll like it, I promise,' Imogen said. 'We're going to climb all the way up into the clouds. Look out the window, little one. Watch and see.' Aurora craned towards the window, her sweet little fingers pressing to the glass.

'Do your parents see her often?' Luca asked, and Imogen recognised what he was doing. Driving the conversation in a parallel direction, subtly shifting it from his family to hers. Irritation barbed beneath her skin but she didn't show it.

'They've been great. Very supportive. But mainly it's Gen who helps out on a day-to-day basis.'

He made a gruff noise.

'Don't be annoyed at her for not liking you.'

He arched a brow. 'Did I say I'm annoyed?'

'You look unimpressed.'

'If I'm unimpressed, Imogen, it's because you had to rely on anyone to help you, rather than turning to me, her father.'

'Oh.' Chastened, she focused all her attention on Aurora, not brave enough to look at him for the anger and disapproval she might see in his eyes. She couldn't bear it. Just like that, the conversation was dead in the water, Imogen's attempts to draw him out flattened by the immutable reality that would always exist between them, no matter what he said to the contrary. He would never really forgive her for keeping Aurora a secret.

And so what?

She'd never forgive him for how he'd treated her, so they were even.

Except they weren't, because no matter how badly he'd hurt Imogen, she knew she was comparing apples and oranges. To keep a baby from a parent seemed, now, like a terrible decision.

But at the time, it had all made sense. She'd weighed up her options and had known Luca wouldn't want to be a father.

Or was it just that she couldn't risk that he might?

That despite all the horribly cruel things he'd said to her, she might have to raise their baby with him at her side anyway? Had she pretended the decision was based on what was best for Luca and Aurora but, in actuality, she'd chosen the path that most suited her?

Her skin was pale as they lifted into the skies, and Imogen only hoped that if Luca noticed, he'd put it down to a slight aversion to air travel and not the ice-cold sensation in her veins, a conviction that she'd made a terrible mistake three years ago—a mistake she could never truly fix.

CHAPTER SEVEN

HIS VILLA IN Tuscany was like something out of a film. Having landed at Pisa Airport, they had been met by a car straight off the plane and driven for about twenty minutes, through stunning vistas of rolling green hills on either side, towards the Ligurian Sea. Eventually, the car had turned off the main road onto a smaller, dusty track lined on one side by enormous pine trees, before turning once more, this time to pass between wide wrought-iron gates. The drive was sweeping and long, showing more of the mesmerising countryside views on one side and an incomparable outlook over where the River Arno met the sea on the other.

From what she could see, the house was surrounded by a large parcel of land, bounded on all sides by those magnificent pine trees. As for the house, it was old and classically Tuscan, with earthy rendered walls, red terracotta tiles and curved architectural features. It was single story and sprawling, and when the car pulled up, an older Italian woman, slim and neatly dressed with her hair in a low ponytail, strode out to meet them.

'My housekeeper,' he explained.

'You have a housekeeper?'

'The villa is well-staffed,' he said. 'It has to be. I don't spend much time here. They take care of things.'

Right on cue, two more staff members appeared, younger men, moving to the trunk to remove their suitcases, so Imogen could focus on lifting Aurora out of her car seat. After the flight and the drive, her little legs were itching to run, and Imogen put her down on the ground.

'Is there anything on the property I need to be aware of?' she asked, turning back to Luca, who was looking at their daughter with that same expression she'd now seen multiple times—as though he'd seen a ghost.

He glanced back at her. 'There's a lake, but it's all the way down there. She'd have to run pretty fast to make it without us realising.'

'Okay, good to know, though. Nothing else?'

He looked around. 'Not that I can think of.'

She watched as Aurora crouched down and ran her hands over the grass then picked a flower—bright pink with lush green leaves—then ran back to Imogen and held it out to her. 'For you, Mama.'

Imogen's heart turned over. 'Thank you, my darling. I love it.' She took the flower and tucked it neatly into the band of her plait.

Luca's voice was gruff. 'I'll show you around.' He strode towards the house, not pausing to see that they were following. Imogen took Aurora's hand rather than lifting her, to give their daughter time to use her legs and also to explore at her own pace, but it meant they lagged behind Luca, and he had to stop and wait for them inside the foyer.

Imogen was glad he'd waited, but not so glad when he began to walk again because she wanted to stop and take everything in.

'This place is incredible,' she said, shaking her head. 'I was about to say it's not what I would have expected for you, but that's not entirely accurate. It's actually… You're perfect here.'

He frowned, his non-comprehension clear.

'You look completely at home. It's as if you were carved from these hills and valleys.' She gestured to the expansive view shown from the living room windows, of the rolling, verdant hills.

'I grew up on the other side of Siena,' he said, and then turned away from her. He clearly regretted giving her that information, that tiny kernel, as if it told her anything fundamental about him! Frustration swirled in her gut, but she didn't push him further.

They walked through the house, which was every bit as charming inside as the outside had indicated. From the large terracotta floor tiles to huge glass windows and furniture that seemed to blend into the surrounds, it was a quintessentially Tuscan home, and Imogen couldn't help but fall a little in love with it.

He left the recording studio until last. They descended a set of stairs, into a basement. 'The wine cellar is that side.' He nodded towards a timber door. 'The recording studio this one.'

'So, if recording is going badly I can wander across and grab a bottle?' she joked.

His smile was tight. Irritation shifted inside her but she opened the door to the recording studio and looked around, then pivoted back to Luca. 'You weren't kidding. This is state of the art.'

'As I've been told.'

They'd arranged for a producer from Florence to join them for a couple of days, while she was recording, and

Imogen was glad she wouldn't have to get to grips with the technical equipment.

The housekeeper—Anna—had made a platter and set it up on one of the terraces that overlooked the ocean side of the property. It was all so beautiful, and, in her heart, Imogen felt a small pang to imagine—for the briefest moment—what it would be like if there were more substance to their relationship.

If they were a real family.

The thought was like acid in her throat. Midway through reaching for an olive, she sat upright, her chest hurting. Growing up, her parents had been blissfully happy, and Imogen had always presumed her life would be like theirs. That she'd meet someone, fall in love, get engaged and married, have babies and live happily ever after. It hadn't seemed like a fairy-tale to her; it had seemed like reality. A bona fide fact of life, in fact. Perhaps that had made her particularly susceptible to the fantasy of Luca. She'd been attracted to him, so it had been easy to tell herself she was falling in love with him, that she loved him—even when she could see now that she didn't really know him. And love couldn't exist when it was one-sided. Not real love. It had to be mutual and shared, and theirs certainly hadn't been.

He had given her a wake-up call that morning, and not just in terms of them as a couple, but in terms of how she viewed life. Her parents' happy relationship, far from being a given, was a gift: a rare, special form of connection and respect that had always made marriage look easy. Imogen knew, now, that wasn't the case.

Life wasn't easy either. It was messy and complex, and Luca had taught her that.

This wasn't real, this wasn't romantic, this wasn't a

family vacation. It was a gesture, from Luca, to help her with her career. She kept that at the front of her mind as they ate, refusing to be seduced by the beauty of the setting or the man sitting opposite her, even when one look at him had the tendency of turning her insides to lava.

He shouldn't have brought her here. He shouldn't have offered up his studio to her. Or, if he had, he should have sent Imogen alone.

Because seeing Imogen and Aurora in Italy was tugging at a part of him he'd had no idea existed. A yearning to come back to Italy, to be *home*.

The same country he'd run hundreds of miles from as soon as he was able, because every glance had reminded him of his parents and sister. How painful those memories had been, how awful his recollections of those happier times, because of their absence.

Every day after the accident had been torturous. All he'd been able to focus on was how badly he'd wanted to escape. How badly he'd *needed* to escape.

And then he'd bought this villa, as yet another form of torture. He'd come here sparingly, when he'd needed a touchstone to his grief, a reminder of why he didn't deserve happiness.

He'd come here after Imogen.

He'd come here when he'd wanted to recommit to his intention.

He was not worthy of love. He could not be trusted with it. He did not deserve happiness.

And yet…seeing Imogen and Aurora here, set against the landscape of his youth, he wasn't sure he knew how to fight this any longer. Not his guilt—that was an incontrovertible part of him.

But so was Aurora.

And even Imogen, because they shared a daughter.

Italy was his home, and in no small part, he wanted it to be Aurora's home too. He wanted to claim this part of her, to make sure it existed.

Because his parents would have wanted that, he realised, a lump forming in his throat unbidden. Nothing would have made them happier than Aurora.

Becoming a father might have been the last thing Luca had ever wanted, but this would have been something his parents desperately longed for.

Didn't he owe it to them—as much as he did his sacrifices and misery—to raise Aurora in line with her heritage?

He closed his eyes as the reality of that twisted and shaped inside of him, altering his understanding of things, and how he must now live. While Luca could never forgive himself for the past, he was no longer an island, able to exist without others, isolated and alone. And he certainly couldn't punish Aurora for his mistakes, nor keep Imogen at a distance because she'd acted out of what she'd mistakenly believed were the best interests of their child.

Could he blame her, given how he'd been at the time? Given what he'd knowingly subjected her to?

A dark groan escaped Luca's throat and he closed his eyes against a rush of realisation. The past had been a noose around his neck for a long time; Luca had no choice but to set it aside, at least partially, to give Aurora the life she deserved. As for Imogen…he had no idea how to navigate their relationship, but he had no choice. He had to try.

The next morning, the sun broke over the Tuscan hillside, bathing Imogen's bedroom in gold and peach, and she pushed back the covers with genuine excitement. She felt like a child on Christmas day. Outside, the valley was every bit as beautiful as it had been the day before, but even more so now because of the dusky light and the clarity of morning. She dressed quickly, checking the time—it was still early—and then moving to Aurora's bedroom. She was still asleep.

Excitement fizzed inside Imogen's belly as she crept into the kitchen and made a cup of tea then moved out onto the terrace, energised by the brush of the crisp morning against her skin, the simple act of sucking air deep into her lungs somehow calming and restorative.

'You're still an early riser.'

His voice was gruff, and close.

She spun around guiltily, cheeks flushed, to see Luca was seated at a round table only a meter or so away, a single shot of very dark coffee before him.

'And you still drink coffee like mud.'

One half of his mouth lifted in a wry smile.

'It's just so beautiful out here. I love the early morning.'

'I remember.'

She looked away, pain in her chest as though she'd been speared with something hot and sharp. She hated that he remembered. She hated that she'd been so unguarded with him, so open and honest. She needed to say something to bring it back to the reality of what had happened, how he'd used her and discarded her when it had suited him.

'Was I unusual?'

She kept her gaze pinned to the valley beyond them.

'In what way?' His voice was casual, easy, but she wasn't fooled. Everything with Luca was a calculation. Reading her before responding.

'In terms of waking early. I guess your usual lovers

were more…sophisticated.' She turned to face him, scanning his face. He sipped his coffee, replaced the cup.

'I don't have a "usual."'

Not *didn't*, she noted, but the present tense. *I don't*.

She wanted to say something acerbic, to pick this fight with him. Despite the beauty of the morning, old pain had surfaced fast and she felt a pull to flex it. But before she could speak, movement caught her eye. He stood, walking towards her with his easy, confident gait. She held her breath, wondering what he would say, how he would continue the conversation. If he might touch her—kiss her. If she might weaken and do so first.

'You're recording today?'

She glanced up at him, frowning. It was a total conversation swerve. She sipped her tea. 'After lunch.'

'Then you're free this morning?'

Her heart stammered. 'Why?'

'I was thinking of taking Aurora to the beach.' He paused. To read her reaction? Or out of uncertainty? 'Join us.'

Imogen ignored the strange sensation of pain, the feeling of being on the other side of that 'us.' She ignored the sense of being excluded, because that was the exact opposite of what he was doing.

Besides, she was here to work. He was trying to facilitate her recording of this demo—by offering her his recording studio, by minding Aurora while she worked. For all his faults, she could hardly charge him with anything new in the present circumstances.

She looked towards the rolling hills, wondering at the stitching sensation in the centre of her chest.

'It's not far. You'll be back in plenty of time.'

It almost sounded like he *wanted* her to go with them.

'You'd be fine without me,' she said, wondering if a fear of being alone with Aurora was at the heart of it. 'I've seen you with her. You're great.'

'This is one of the most beautiful coves in the world—though having grown up near here, I might be a little biased. Even at this time of year, it's worth the trip, though I wouldn't recommend swimming.' He was quiet, thoughtful. 'I thought you might like to see it. But of course, the choice is yours.'

Well, now she felt a little silly. She sipped her tea, torn between going with her heart, which was telling her, *Heck, yes! Explore and enjoy!* and her mind, which was shouting at her, *Steer clear, you can't trust him!*

She angled a glance at him, wariness in the lines of her face.

'I'll come. But only to see the beach.'

He nodded once. No smile, but something warmed her in the middle of her chest, and she realised, after he'd left, that it was the *way* he'd looked at her. The same way he'd looked at her back then that had made her feel like she was the very centre of his world, his eyes laced with such admiration she could hardly blink away. He was like a solar eclipse—impossible to look back at without getting burned. Only, back then, that very same look had made her believe they were in love. It had been a lie—something she would remember this time around.

They left the villa as soon as Aurora woke, which was not long after their conversation on the terrace. Imogen only had time to pack a beach bag with some towels, hats, spare clothes and some snacks for Aurora before Luca was propelling them out the door towards his garage. When he opened it, she realised he had not just the four-wheel drive that had driven them yesterday, but a fleet of cars secured in here, including a sleek sports car with a soft top. And naturally, he'd had car seats installed in several.

She glanced across at him, a teasing expression on her features, but he simply shrugged and set about securing Aurora into the back of the sports car, leaving Imogen to settle herself in the front passenger seat.

Halfway to the beach, he pulled off the road, turning into a sleepy-looking town that was so wonderfully Tuscan.

Imogen took at least a hundred photos with her phone as they drove through it. Cobbled streets, higgledy-piggledy rendered houses, flowerpots overflowing with rosemary and lavender, window baskets with geraniums spilling down towards the ground, laundry strung from one window to another, and little shops set up with artful displays of fruit and vegetables. He pulled over near one of these shops, turned to Imogen and asked, 'Hungry?'

She was. They hadn't had time for breakfast, and besides the snacks she'd packed for Aurora, food hadn't occurred to her.

He disappeared into a bar and returned a few minutes later with some paper bags and a couple of take-away coffees. She salivated as the aroma hit her nostrils and peeked into the bags to see a couple of flatbreads that were overwhelmingly garlicky, with red tomato sauce oozing into the melted cheese.

At the beach, she spread out some towels and they sat side by side, eating their *piadina* and watching as Aurora delightedly played in the sand. She ran it through her fingers, pressed it to her cheeks, pushed it around to make different shapes.

'She's never been to the seaside before,' Imogen admitted, halfway through her flatbread.

Luca tilted a glance at her. She felt the heat of his inspection, his curiosity, and found herself letting down barriers she'd sworn she'd keep in place. Because he was here, and he'd bought her the most delicious breakfast ever. Because he'd suggested this outing. Or maybe because she felt relaxed, for the first time in a long time? Wasn't that a problem, though? To relax around Luca was the first step towards forgetting, and she couldn't forget.

'Why not?'

She'd been silent for long enough that he'd been led to probe further. 'No time or opportunity,' she said after a pause. 'We've travelled to my parents', for Christmases, birthdays, that kind of thing. They live in the Cotswolds, so that's kind of become our go-to holiday destination. It's beautiful, and free, so it ticks all the boxes.'

He nodded thoughtfully, but said nothing.

'Did you come here, growing up?'

The air crackled. Imogen could have sworn she saw a spark. She'd asked him about something she knew he didn't want to discuss, but so what? Why shouldn't she get to return volley?

'From time to time.'

It was classic Luca: evasive and dismissive, all at once. But Imogen remembered. She remembered how angry she'd been after he'd dumped her, for not pushing him harder. For not making him open up to her. Maybe if she had, she'd have understood him better sooner. Been able to save herself.

'What does that mean?'

'It means occasionally.'

'With your parents? Friends?'

'My parents, and my aunt and uncle. My cousins occasionally. Friends.'

She had to concentrate on not rolling her eyes. He'd listed just about everyone under the sun, which had given her no real impression of what his life had been like in Italy.

'Did you like to swim, as a boy?'

He had only a small piece of *piadina* left. 'What boy doesn't?' He finished his flatbread then scrunched up the paper bag, holding it in the palm of one hand. Nearby, Aurora had stopped playing with sand and was now staring at a pair of seagulls squawking towards the shore, their beaks doing frequent inspections of the wet sand, hoping to strike gold.

'What else did you do?'

He was quiet, moving the scrunched-up paper from one hand to another.

'At the beach?'

'As a boy.'

'Typical stuff. Football. Hikes. Skiing in winter.'

Her smile was wry, but in the back of her mind, she felt a slight tremor, a thrill, because he'd told her *something* that was real, something biographical. Not that it was particularly interesting or important, but it was a start.

And why do you care? a voice challenged.

She was supposed to be keeping him at a distance, not trying to drill down into his past. And yet…he was the father of her child. There was some common sense in getting to know him more deeply: a necessity now, more than it ever was before.

'Not so typical for someone like me,' she said.

'No? You hiked, as a child.' There it was again. The imbalance. His memory of her, his knowledge, because she'd shared so openly and willingly in that month they'd spent together.

'Yes. I still do, when I can.'

He nodded slowly. 'My father taught me to hike. Not in parks, but rather in the wild. He showed me how to read the weather, look for predators' tracks, find food if necessary.'

'He sounds like a natural outdoorsman.'

Luca was saved from replying by Aurora, who wandered over to them with a look of such excitement it was as if she'd won some kind of lottery. She held in her tiny hand a shell that was picture book perfect, curved and a deep silvery brown in colour. 'Look!' she squealed. 'Mama, look!'

Imogen smiled indulgently, taking the shell in one hand and examining it. 'That's very pretty, Aurora.'

She handed it to Luca to inspect. He took it, looked inside, then gestured for Aurora to come closer. 'Let me show you something,' he said, and the little girl trustingly settled herself into Luca's lap, pulling at every single one of Imogen's heartstrings. He held the shell towards her ear, but she spun to look at it.

'No, no,' he said, gently though, and with a smile that made Imogen's eyes sting, because he'd never smiled at her with that look of simple pleasure. Her heart hurt. She glanced away quickly, pulling hair behind her ears and blinking rapidly, before turning back in time to see him press the shell to Aurora's ear.

'Do you hear it?' he asked, watching the little girl's face flicker with emotions.

'Ocean!' She pointed towards the water.

'Yes.' He smiled again. Imogen too, but her own was wistful. Despite the simplistic beauty of that moment, she couldn't help but feel sad. Sad at what Luca had missed out on—and what Aurora had likewise. Because she'd made a decision based on her experiences of him. She'd judged him by how he'd treated her, as though that defined him. As though that meant he was only capable of cruelty, when in fact, towards his daughter, he was capable of...love.

Yes, love. She saw it on his face now and almost gasped. She had the strangest sense that Aurora and Luca had formed a bubble, and for the first time since Aurora's birth, Imogen felt like an outsider with her own daughter. She stuffed the rest of her *piadina* into her mouth, but could no longer enjoy the complex, savoury flavours.

'Mama, listen. Mama!'

Imogen turned back to Aurora and took the shell, held it to her ears and listened.

'My mother used to say it was a way of bringing the beach home. She always hated leaving, and so I would collect these shells for her, so she could listen no matter where she was.'

Imogen's heart twisted. Before she could answer, Luca was standing, dislodging Aurora, whose little hand he clasped in his. 'Come on, *bella*. Let's go feel the water in our toes.'

Luca had found himself dreading Aurora's bedtime that night. When their daughter was with them, it was easy to focus on her, to distract himself and stay busy with the child they shared. It was easy to watch her and laugh at her and focus all his energy on her needs. But when Aurora was dispensed with for the night, it left him and Imogen here, in a place he now recognised was incredibly beautiful and...romantic.

Romantic.

God, he'd never thought of it that way before. This had always just been a good investment. A place he'd got cheap because the rock star who'd owned it had lost their fortune, come on hard times and needed to sell. Luca had paid above the asking and still got it for a steal. He'd bought it because it made solid financial sense, and he'd always viewed it through that lens.

But Imogen being here gave the place a different kind of life. It gave it a whole new light and air, a vibe that he'd never noticed before. Even the sunlight had hit the house differently from the moment they'd arrived.

It was Aurora, too, he admitted, pouring himself a glass of local red wine and cradling it in his hand, stepping out onto the terrace and looking towards the now ink-black sea. He had known she was his daughter from the moment he'd seen her. She was instantly familiar to him. But seeing her here, in Tuscany, he'd had the sense of bringing her home. Where she belonged.

Where he belonged.

Something cracked in the centre of his chest.

A pain. A comprehension. A sense of dread.

He'd left Italy on his eighteenth birthday, turning his back completely on the uncle and aunt who'd cared for him after his parents' deaths, ignoring them to the point of callousness; turning his back on everything that reminded him of how much he'd lost, and who he'd been before. He came here sparingly, as a form of punishment. When he wanted to be most pained by the past, he visited Tuscany and he wallowed in his memories, in reflections of how perfect his life had once been.

But seeing Aurora here, dangerous promises were

whispering to him. Seductive, tantalising temptations, like: *What if it could be perfect again?*

He knew it couldn't be, though. It never would be. Even if, somehow, he could find happiness with Imogen and Aurora, he would never let himself enjoy it.

Being here with them was an added form of torture— that was all. Seeing Imogen smile, hearing her joke and laugh and watching her cuddle Aurora, who was as Italian as the day was long, made him want to forget his past. But Luca never would. Nor would he forget his failures and his grief. A mistake had defined him as a twelve-year-old; nothing would ever change that.

And yet, even knowing he didn't deserve happiness in life, there were other things he had started to realise. Such as the vulnerable position he was currently in. Imogen had moved in with him, for Aurora, to ease this transition, and because Luca had insisted upon it.

They weren't a family, but at the same time, they were. For Aurora's sake, shouldn't they strive to be? Shouldn't they try to give her something like he'd known as a child? Like Imogen had known? This wasn't about them, their attraction, nor their history. Everything now hinged on the present, and the future they wanted to create for Aurora.

They'd made the outing to the beach work.

It had been pleasant.

More than pleasant, it had been… He searched for a word and found he couldn't come up with one to describe it. The trip had been spontaneous but also…perfect. Cathartic, perhaps. He'd loved seeing Aurora discover the things he'd discovered and adored as a child. He'd felt a heavy connection to his parents, being there with his own child, feeling things they must have felt. He wasn't just walking in their footsteps; he was being shepherded by them. Never had he felt their presence so keenly.

He'd loved seeing Imogen there as well. He'd loved watching her watch Aurora, seeing the adoration on her face, knowing that despite everything that had happened between them, Aurora was a gift. A gift he hadn't asked for, but one he wasn't stupid enough to take for granted.

If anything, he'd been bowled over by how much Aurora had flooded his heart—a heart he'd sworn was cut off from the world, and would be for all time. The total, possessive love he felt for her, because she was *his* child, to love and protect. He was her father, a role that he knew to be sacred and important, because of how his own father had been. Atoning for the past by denying his own happiness had always been a driving force for Luca, but now there was an equally important goal in his mind: to be everything Aurora needed him to be. He would be a real father to her—not just a temporary dad, but someone who was there, day and night, whenever she wanted his advice or presence.

Yet an uneasiness crept through him as he acknowledged how temporary this situation might prove to be. He had no idea what Imogen's life had been like in the last few years, but he'd seen her that night at the bar with another man, had seen her hug him and smile at him, and he'd felt everything slipping with the realisation that other men saw her as he did, wanted her as he did.

That had been *before* he'd known about Aurora. What would happen if Imogen met someone now—if she started dating, fell in love and married, and Aurora then had a stepdad? On the one hand, Luca recognised that the pain of that would serve him right—an excellent punishment for having let his family die.

Even he couldn't go that far, though. Though punishing himself was a long-held habit, too much was at stake now to lean into those patterns. He had to protect this world they were building, this mirage of a family. He had to make sure this lasted, for Aurora's sake alone...

CHAPTER EIGHT

AFTER A LONG and immensely satisfying session in the studio, Imogen wanted company. No, she wanted Luca's company, she admitted to herself, in a way that she knew she should resist. And yet, she approached the terrace, where Luca stood, but she hesitated before stepping out onto it.

In London, they'd established a rhythm that worked for them. A sort of truce that made it possible to juggle the complexity of their arrangement. But here, in Tuscany, it was different. He was different and she was different; even Aurora was different.

It was a special place, the kind of home that invited magic to dance in the air around them, so a sense of awe and awkwardness swirled through Imogen as she stood just inside the villa, looking out at Luca's back. But he was still the same Luca. Even when she glimpsed something vulnerable in him, even when he said something that made her wonder about him on a deeply human level, she knew what he was capable of. And it didn't much matter what had caused him to be the way he was. He'd always be capable of repeating the callous way he'd treated her before. He'd always be capable of hurting her. She'd be stupid to let her guard down, even somewhere like this that invited true, heartfelt intimacy.

That wasn't what she wanted from him. It wasn't something they could ever achieve—not after their past.

So when she stepped onto the terrace, it was with a grim expression and a certainty that despite the beauty of their surroundings, the relationship between them was rotten at its core.

Perhaps to remind them both of that, she asked him something she'd wondered for a long time, though hadn't ever really planned to bring up. 'How soon after I left did you replace me anyway, Luca?'

It certainly set the tone for their conversation. Just like that, she'd wiped away the pleasant day and evening they'd spent and had plunged them back into the sparkling animosity of three years, or even two weeks, ago.

He turned to face her, his expression giving nothing away. The moon was high and full, shining and white, and it cast his symmetrical face into a shadow.

'It's not a tough question,' she said when he didn't respond.

'No, it's not. And yet I doubt you want the answer.'

Her stomach dropped to her toes. She turned towards the view, sucking in a sharp breath. He hadn't answered, and yet he had. He'd basically confirmed what she'd feared and hated most at the time. He'd moved on straightaway. He'd replaced her straightaway. She had been dispensable to him. *Replaceable*.

Her heart hurt.

Not because she still cared for him, but because she had then. She'd cared for him, loved him in an open and innocent way, and he'd discarded her like a nobody. She forced herself to be strong, to keep her back straight when she felt like slumping, to keep her features expressionless when she halfway wanted to cry.

'I'm interested as to why you would ask.'

'I've wondered about it over the years, that's all.'

Silence fell, staticky and sharp. Imogen curled her hands around the railing, her throat hurting with the emotions she was containing.

'Did you truly not realise that I thought I was falling in love with you?'

More silence. 'I saw what I wanted to see,' he admitted.

'Which was?'

'Us being on the same page.'

'We weren't.'

'I know that now.'

She swallowed. 'I can't be the first woman who's claimed to love you.'

She glanced at him to see him frown thoughtfully. 'You were.'

'But not the first woman to feel it. Or to think she felt it,' she corrected quickly, the distinction an important one for her pride.

'Believe me, Imogen, what happened between us was a one off. I don't sleep with virgins. I don't sleep with anyone for weeks on end.'

'Then why me?' she pushed, his revelation doing something funny to her stomach, making it twist and loop.

'You know the answer to that,' he responded, a tone in his voice that spoke of repressed anger and impatience.

'Spell it out for me,' she demanded.

He glared at her and then moved quickly, his mouth seeking hers, taking it, crushing it, demanding her submission. A submission she gave all too willingly, her body pliant against his, the emotions of the last few days, of the last few weeks, building up to an enormous fountain of need that was erupting between them both.

'This is your answer,' he groaned, moving his hand to her back and pushing her towards him. 'I don't know why, but from the first moment we met, I haven't been able to resist you. I had to have you then, and God, I want to have you now. I want to have you always, Imogen. Do you understand that? You are a fire in my blood, a need that overtakes all of my senses. You are a drug to which I am addicted, and I hate you for that, even when I know I would give my life for yours.'

She was breathless from passion and confusion. His words almost sounded like a declaration of love, but they weren't. There was a darkness to them, an anger, a resentment and bitterness, as though wanting her was the worst thing that had ever happened to him.

She pulled back to look at him, needing to see, to understand, but he kissed her again, and this time, he lifted her, bringing her with him back inside the villa, to the rug by the unlit fire, laying her down and kissing her while his knee wedged between her legs and his body lay heavily on hers, moving just enough to awaken every single one of her senses. Except common sense, which had deserted her the moment their lips connected.

'Do you understand what you do to me?' he ground out, pushing her shirt up to reveal her bra and then lifting her breast over the cup, exposing her nipple to his hungry gaze and then his desperate mouth, which ravaged her until she was moaning and arching her back on spasm after spasm of pleasure—pleasure so intense it was a form of torture in and of itself.

His hand curved around her bottom, lifting her to meet his arousal, and she whimpered, fully convinced that if he didn't take her now she might crumble and die. 'Please,' she moaned, over and over, her hands pushing at his clothes impatiently while he reached for protection and unfurled it over his length. She wore a skirt, and he reached underneath it to find her underwear, sliding them down her legs and pushing the skirt up, entering her without even undressing her; such was their need, mutual and hungry.

She whimpered with gladness as he filled her and her muscles squeezed around him, her whole body trembling with the gift of her first release. She curled her legs around his waist as he began to move once more, and again and again she rode a wave of ecstasy, until finally he joined her, his voice thick and dark in the room, his convulsions echoing her own tidal euphoria.

He pressed his head into the curve of her neck and then pushed up onto his elbows so he could see her properly.

'Listen, Imogen.' His voice was hoarse, his breath still coming in fits from their exertions. 'I need to talk to you.'

Her heart stammered; dread filled her veins with ice. 'What about?'

'This.'

Her lips parted. She didn't pretend to misunderstand. 'Us?'

His brows knit together. If he denied there was an 'us,' she was scared she might slap him. He was still atop her, inside her, filling her senses and body with his presence; she wouldn't let him sideline her again.

'I like you.'

Her heart stammered. It was an underwhelming declaration, especially after the need he'd professed to feel for her moments earlier, and yet it was doing something strange to her insides, churning them up and making them unrecognisable.

'I respect you.'

Her pulse rushed.

'And I think you are a very good mother.'

Warmth slid through her. She bit into her lip, fighting a strange urge to cry. Her hand lifted up and pressed to his chest, connecting with the solid wall of his pectoral muscles and the heavy thudding of his heart.

'I do not want to hurt you again, Imogen.'

Her eyes fluttered shut. It was an admission that came close to being an apology. It was an acceptance of what he'd done to her that she'd badly needed to hear.

'You won't. I'm different now.'

'I can see that.' There was a strange heaviness to his tone. Guilt? Well, that would make sense. Imogen had become cautious because of him. It was his treatment of her that had driven her to view people with mistrust, to overcome her natural instincts and be wary wherever possible.

'I don't love you.'

She gasped. It was one of the most hurtful things she'd ever been told, and that was saying something. They'd just made love, after all.

'I am not saying that to be cruel—I am, in fact, trying to protect you.'

'To protect me from what?' she demanded with hauteur.

'From misunderstanding me.'

'You're being pretty damned clear,' she muttered.

'I would like us to get married.'

It was the very last thing she'd expected him to say. Her whole body trembled and her skin lifted in goose bumps. It was a proposal she'd dreamed of, over countless nights, because her sleeping thoughts were well beyond her control. Everything stopped. The ticking clock above the mantel, the shimmering moon, the rolling waves of the ocean, the rustling grape vines, the night birds flapping their wings, the earth spinning in its place. Everything stopped and fell silent.

'What did you say?'

'Aurora deserves that from us. She deserves the certainty of a real family.'

'I can't... I—'

But he pressed a finger to her lips, silencing her with the intensity of his stare. 'Our marriage would be for Aurora, but that's not to say we would not find a silver lining to it,' he promised. And he moved his hips a little, reminding her that he was still a part of her, and damn it, her body flushed with ready, all-encompassing heat. 'Be my wife, Imogen. Sleep in my bed, night after night. Be mine.' And he kissed her in a way that almost made her think he meant it, that he wanted her to be his wife, even when he'd just told her, in no uncertain terms, that none of this was about her. Not really.

'Stop. Just stop.'

Now she found the strength to push him away, or maybe he simply accepted her need in that moment for space, and acquiesced to it. Luca pulled back, standing, disappearing briefly before returning while still in the process of straightening his clothes.

Imogen sat where she was on the floor, her nerves rioting. 'Did you actually just suggest we get married, after everything we've been through?'

He put his hands into his pockets, looking down at her with a face that was carefully wiped of expression. And she hated that! How easily he could conceal his feelings— if he even had any.

'It makes sense.'

'About as much sense as a polar bear in the Sahara,' she disputed passionately. 'You can't be serious.'

'Why not?'

'Because—because—look at us!' she spat. 'Besides sex, tell me one good thing about our relationship.'

'Aurora.'

Imogen rolled her eyes. 'I'm her mum, you're her dad. We don't have to get married to keep performing those functions.'

'You grew up with the security of two parents who loved one another very much, who doted on you and left you no room for doubt about your place in the world. Tell me that didn't help shape who you are as a person.'

'But it was also their love for one another. Their obvious respect and openness. Seeing their relationship made me want, for myself, a fraction of their happiness.' Her chin jutted defiantly. 'I will never have that with you, and I'm not marrying for anything less.'

For just a flash, she saw his reaction. A visible expression of some dark emotion she couldn't fathom and then he was Luca again, impenetrable, confident, assured. 'We are her parents, and we should be with her. Both of us.'

Imogen pressed her fingers to her temples, shaking her head a little. 'That's crazy. It makes literally no sense.'

'On the contrary, it's the only sensible option.' He moved across to Imogen and crouched down, so their eyes were level. 'I want to make this work, for both of us. Tell me what you would need to consider this.'

Her gut twisted. The answer to that was oh-so-simple and oh-so-terrifying: love. But she didn't love Luca and never would, so why would she want him to love her? Because she wanted her parents' happiness? Or because it was how she'd been raised—to believe that marriage was the ultimate expression of romantic love? It didn't have to be, though. It could be an expression of a parent's love for their child—such as in this instance. Marrying to give the baby stability and the permanence of a family home.

'Lots of people raise children in shared homes,' she said, fighting herself now. 'It's old-fashioned to think we need to be married to do this right.'

'Lots of people do, and I commend them,' he agreed. 'But you and I both want the same version of a family for our daughter. I know that is true.'

She scanned his face. 'Why do you want it, Luca?'

'I've told you—'

'No,' she interrupted quickly, shaking her head with impatience. 'I know what you're *saying*, but that's not the whole answer. It's not the complete truth. What makes you think marriage is such a worthy institution?'

He was silent.

'You never speak about your parents,' she insisted. 'And yet you know all about mine. You know how happy they are, how much that influenced me, because I told you, years ago. But I don't know anything about your parents' relationship and how that shaped you. If I had to go off your reaction to me, though, I would guess something happened to turn you off the whole idea of love and romance at some point in your life. So why this about-face?'

'Our marriage isn't about either of those things.'

'Then it's not a marriage,' she responded, pulling away a little and moving to stand, glad to stretch her legs and gain some space. 'Were they unhappy, Luca? Is that why you were so cruel to me three years ago?'

'That had nothing to do with them,' he responded, but his hand slashed through the air in a way that made her think she was getting to the heart of something. Some truth he wanted, desperately, to keep from her.

'Did they fight?'

'I was a thirty-year-old man when we met, more than old enough to have had my own experiences to take into account.'

'So, it was a woman then? Someone who broke your heart and made you swear off relationships?'

A muscle jerked in his jaw. 'I am not here to be psycho-analysed. We're discussing the prospect of our marriage.'

'There is no prospect of our marriage,' she replied in-stantly. 'Not when you're so intractable. You can't even tell me the most basic information about yourself. You keep everything locked up, hidden away. If I agreed to your proposal, I'd wake up one day and find that I had married a stranger. I'm not going to be surprised by you twice, Luca.'

Silence arced between them. He strode towards her and she held her ground, staring up into his face, daring him to keep arguing with her. He stopped short a few inches away, his eyes holding hers, his features a tight mask of control.

When he spoke, it was with a voice she barely recog-nised. Low and throaty, his accent thicker than usual. 'My mother and father were, like your parents, very happy. They laughed and loved with total abandon. I knew myself to be their ultimate pride. When I was nine, my mother discovered she was pregnant—it had not been planned, but was a welcome surprise. To all of us. We adored An-gelica. Our angel. She was the most beautiful little girl.' His lips twisted into a ghost-like smile. 'So like Aurora.'

He shook his head, the memory clearly painful. She resisted the temptation to reach out and console him by touching his arm. It was a strange barrier after the intimacy they'd just shared, but something held her immobile.

'For my twelfth birthday, we went away together, as a family, to a cabin in the Italian Alps. My parents felt they'd been neglecting me, since Angelica's arrival. They wanted to make a fuss. My father took me out one on one; we hiked, played cards.'

Imogen blinked up at Luca, struggling to reconcile this image of him with the man she knew. The man who'd cut her heart into a thousand little pieces as though it were nothing.

'On the night of my birthday, we had dinner together. I went to my room afterwards—I'd been given some new football trading cards and wanted to sort them.' Another smile, less grim this time. Nostalgic and sad. Her fingers itched to touch him. 'I fell asleep, but awoke sometime later to a loud crash.'

Even if she spoke, she suspected he wouldn't hear. He wasn't really talking to her now, but rather replaying events like a film in his mind, recounting things exactly as they'd happened. And Imogen braced, because it was abundantly clear this wasn't going anywhere happy.

'It was a beam in the lounge room. The fire had not been fully extinguished, and a spark leapt from it to the rug and quickly caught fire. It didn't take long for the whole cabin to be alight. I was down the other end to my parents and Angelica—she was not a good sleeper. They wanted to spare me from that. I tried to get to them, but a beam fell on me.' He ran his fingers over his side distractedly.

Even with his shirt on, she could see the scars there. The delicate bunching of his otherwise perfect skin, the ripples that had always fascinated her. She'd asked about them once; he'd demurred, and she'd let it be.

'I passed out. The next thing I knew, I was being dragged from the cabin by neighbours. They saved me. I was hurt but alive. I wanted to go back in, to save my parents and sister. I could see how badly their section of the house was burning. I needed to get to them. I cried out, I pushed, but the neighbours held me back.'

Tears slipped down Imogen's cheeks.

'I was weak.'

'Weak,' she whispered, askance. 'How?'

His eyes lanced hers. 'I should have been able to reach them. Do you have any idea how many times I have re-played that moment in my mind? There is no force on earth that should have held me where I was. My father had spent the whole trip teaching me to be a man, talking to me about responsibilities and courage, and yet, in that moment of truth, I failed him. I failed them all.'

She gasped, her heart hurting for him now, and not herself. 'No, Luca, no. How can you say that? You were a boy of twelve, you'd been injured, there was a raging fire, and you were being physically restrained.'

'I was afraid,' he muttered, clearly disgusted with him-self. 'I fought to go to them, but I was simultaneously ter-rified. Maybe that's why I let them restrain me? Maybe if I hadn't been afraid, I would have been able to free my-self and run back in?'

'And then what? Do you think there's any possibility you would have survived?' A muscle jerked in his cheek. 'Do you think your parents would have wanted you to die trying to save them?'

'I should have saved them.' His eyes showed such awful

torment. Imogen acted then, putting a hand on his chest, where his heart thumped hard against her palm.

'You couldn't have. You were pinned by a beam. The fire had reached their bedrooms. What happened was a terrible tragedy, but it was not your fault.'

'Do you know what else my father did on that trip, to encourage me to become a man? A man he could be proud of?' Luca said, the words ice-cold.

Imogen shook her head a little.

'He gave me tasks. Responsibilities. "Every person in a family carries their weight, my boy."'

A shiver of presentiment ran the length of Imogen's spine.

'One of my *duties*—' he almost spat the word '—was to extinguish the fire each night. But I was too excited by my football cards to do it properly. I rushed. I didn't check. I just wanted to sort through the damned things.'

Imogen's face scrunched up. 'That's not your fault.'

'Are you kidding? It's the definition of "my fault."'

'Listen to me, Luca. Listen to me properly a moment. If your father was anything like mine, he was always there, a shadow, like training wheels, guiding you when I needed it, but always, always checking on you. There is no way, absolutely none, that your father would have given you a task as important as that and not checked you had done it. Particularly not on your birthday, when it's entirely predictable that you would be distracted by your gifts.'

Luca's eyes closed. It was clear that while he'd heard her words, he didn't want to take them on.

'You knew him. Am I wrong?'

A muscle jerked in his jaw. 'There is no defence for what I did, and then failed to do. None.'

She felt as though she were being handed the keys to

something important—she just couldn't quite work out what. It didn't matter, though. This was about him, not her understanding of him.

She stroked his chest gently, letting her fingers move to his sides. 'You were just a boy.'

His Adam's apple shifted as he swallowed, visibly regrouping. 'After that night, the lights went out for me. But before that, my life was... I saw what you saw. My parents were in love, yes, and more than that, Angelica and I were their reasons for being. Nothing made them prouder or happier than when we simply walked into the room.'

Her heart was thumping into her ribs.

'I would like our daughter to know that feeling.'

Imogen groaned softly.

She wanted that too. She wanted them to raise Aurora together, to be able to make this work. She was far from believing marriage to be a prerequisite for raising a child together. She'd been doing it alone for more than two years, and she'd met heaps of single mum and dads, and couples of all sorts of configurations—married, engaged, never planning to marry, gay, straight. She had no preconceptions about what a modern family looked like. All that mattered to Imogen was what was right for *them*—for their family, and for them as individuals.

For the briefest fraction of time, she was tempted to simply say *yes* and work out the details later. The old Imogen would have. The Imogen he'd first met, three years ago, who'd taken everyone on faith, who'd loved without boundaries, who'd believed the best about people and life. But she'd learned her lesson, she'd taken it to heart, and it was wrapped around her now, protecting her even when her old nature wanted to reassert itself.

'I understand why you've suggested this, and I'm not

going to lie and say I'm not open to considering it.' His eyes probed hers, his face back to a blank mask of control. 'But I need to think about it, about everything.' She lowered her hand further, to catch his with hers. 'Just give me some time.'

CHAPTER NINE

EVERYTHING WAS DIFFERENT NOW. She still hated him—at least, she hated what he'd done to her, how he'd treated her—but she pitied him too, and she ached for him. She now *knew* him in the way she'd been wanting to know him all this time. More than knowing small details about him, she *understood* him.

His pain was such that one could not easily recover from it. His pain was a burden he'd carried since he was twelve, and it had shaped him, formed him, formed his beliefs and opinions, his thoughts about himself.

'Oh, Luca,' she sighed wistfully, because it was all so very sad. She went to bed thinking about him, and woke the next morning in the same headspace, but Luca was back to being Luca—closed off, acting as though they were polite acquaintances. Acting as though he hadn't asked her to marry him the night before.

It drove her wild, but a new level of sensitivity had entered her thoughts, and so she let it go, treating him with the same cool reserve as she made a cup of tea. Aurora woke, and they spent the morning exploring the grounds of the villa, but the vibe was completely different from the day before. Imogen hung back, allowing father and daughter to bond, to spend time together, to get to know one another.

The same sense that she was an outsider to their bubble permeated Imogen. His marriage proposal twisted in her mind. At first, she'd dismissed it as impossible. It was an idea so totally out of left field that she'd been blindsided. Yet it wasn't totally unrealistic.

'Tell me what you need to make this work.'

That was a good question. What did she need? He was obviously an excellent father, but would he continue to have this kind of time for Aurora when life resumed a more normal routine? It was still a novelty. What if she agreed to marry him and found that he became as unavailable to Aurora as he had been to Imogen during their relationship? Somehow, back then, he'd subtly created the expectation that his days were his own, and she hadn't even noticed, far less minded. She'd come to care for him, to rely on him being a part of her life, and he'd let her down. What if he let Aurora down too?

Did she want to be married to someone who was capable of partitioning her and Aurora so completely from his life?

But why did she think he'd do that with Aurora? How he'd treated Imogen had nothing to do with his decisions as a father. It was, nonetheless, something to discuss with him—what did he imagine his role would be? What would this possible marriage even look like? Who would have what responsibilities?

Out of nowhere, she saw Genevieve's face and shivered, because her twin sister had been her guiding light for so much of her life. Genevieve's judgement was flawless—and she would not condone even the discussion of a marriage to Luca. She'd tell Imogen to scoop Aurora up and run a mile.

Only, Genevieve hadn't really seen Luca with Aurora. Not for more than a few hours when she'd come to help out, and Imogen was pretty sure that just by her presence, she would have changed the dynamic. She also didn't know Luca, outside of how he'd made Imogen feel three years earlier. That wasn't unimportant, but it also wasn't everything.

Wasn't it?

Imogen stopped walking, frowning. Was she actually starting to let that pain go? To admit that it wasn't the be-all and end-all of the lens through which she should see Luca?

She couldn't. Self-preservation made her cling to it, to remember the hurt, his coldness, his awful dismissal of her.

But it was overlaid by his confession the night before. His throaty, raw voice as he'd talked about his parents, and losing them, and how he felt he'd failed his whole family. Had he got professional help back then, to deal with his grief? Had he spoken to anyone about it since?

A breeze rustled past, cold enough to make her shiver and wrap her denim jacket more tightly around her frame, her fingers lingering over her flat stomach.

Aurora had grown in there. New life, Luca and Imogen's child, and Imogen had felt their baby inside of her, swirling and swishing around. She had known and loved Aurora for almost as long as her heart had been shattered by Luca. Every decision she'd made in life from the moment she discovered she was pregnant, had been in Aurora's best interests.

For their daughter, she would do anything—even step back into the lion's den.

Only, he didn't seem like such a lion now—or at least, she couldn't see the lion without also recognising the cub he'd once been, badly hurt by events in his life, and unable to escape their long, dark shadows.

Shadows, though, were not impenetrable. She watched as Aurora said something, pointed and clapped and Luca crouched down to lift her up, holding her higher, so she could see the fruit on the tree. She touched it, and Luca nodded and smiled, so his eyes creased at the corners. Imogen's pulse ratchetted up.

Aurora had been named with care, for the Roman goddess of dawn, because Imogen had known she would be just that: a new dawn after so much bleak sadness and grief. And she had been.

Aurora had been her dawn, her morning light, her sunshine and warmth, and as she watched father and daughter together, she had no doubt she would be for Luca as well. And Imogen smiled at the exact same moment he turned to look for her, so their eyes met, and her heart flooded with warmth, as a new hope crested inside of her once more. Genevieve's warning was forgotten—for now at least.

After two days of recording, Imogen had laid down enough tracks for a decent demo, and the producer had promised to get the finished files to her the following week. Luca insisted on dinner on the terrace to celebrate, and Imogen found she couldn't refuse. The sky was dark with hints of mauve lingering like streaks, whispers of dusk and the day that had passed. The stars were shining, and the trees formed perfect silhouettes, reminding Imogen of the picture books she'd read as a child.

It was nothing to the terrace itself though, as ancient as it was beautiful, with the hip-height columns forming a railing over which ivy had begun to scramble many years earlier, covering it now with verdant green tendrils. The table had been set with white linen and a candle sat in the middle, only just lit, so it was still tall and proud, casting them in a flickering golden light, and an ice bucket held a bottle of expensive champagne, the cork already removed.

'It's really not worth celebrating yet,' she said, shaking her head a little. 'Not until the demo's been sent in and they like it.'

He poured her a glass of champagne regardless, then lifted his own to salute it. 'Have you done this before?'

She shook her head a little. 'Not specifically. I recorded a couple of demos when Aurora was much younger.'

'And?'

She flushed pink, remembering the day she'd got the call from the major label. 'I sold one of the songs.'

'You sold a song?'

'It was the sound they'd been looking for, for one of their artists. I was in a fog of looking after Aurora, I was exhausted, and then this call came through—I couldn't believe it.'

He was quiet, watchful.

'It all happened so fast. One minute, I'm signing a contract, and the next, the song was on the airwaves. It was the strangest feeling, to hear my words, my music, being sung by someone else.'

'That's an incredible achievement. You must have been so proud.'

She tilted her head a little. 'I was a thousand things. Proud, excited, shocked, overwhelmed.'

'Have you sold anything since?'

'I haven't wanted to. I was flattered and excited—to have a bona fide pop star singing my song was such a rush. But it's *my* song, and I want to be the one to sing my songs. If I can.' She gestured towards the house, where the recording studio was situated. 'This is my dream. I know it's a long shot, but I have to at least try.'

'It's not a long shot,' he denied, shifting his gaze thoughtfully to his champagne flute, as if transfixed by the bubbles rioting inside the fine glass. 'The first night I heard you sing, I was transported. Your voice is ethereal and at the same time completely grounding. I didn't know, until I heard you sing, that music could make you *feel*, deep in your soul.'

She stared at him, a thousand feelings exploding through her. He'd praised her singing before, but now she understood why he almost seemed to resent the impact her voice had on him. So much of Luca was an act—an effort to keep himself from showing pleasure, so that he couldn't feel it. To keep himself walled off. Sympathy softened her.

'You have a beautiful voice,' he said, without expanding further.

She stifled a small sigh, but wrapped his praise in her memories. 'If I can't get a deal, I'll just keep doing what I'm doing. Teaching and singing gigs. I love that too, you know. Connecting with an audience, watching them sing along and dance, it's very rewarding.' She sipped her champagne. 'Anyway, we'll see what comes of this.'

'What's the label?'

She named a big American-based company. 'One of

their executives has been coming to watch me sing for a few months now. We've become friends, I guess. He's really supportive and thinks I have a good chance.'

Luca was still, his eyes probing hers, as if remembering something, or thinking it. 'Tall guy? Dark hair, beard?'

She frowned. 'How did you know?'

His laugh was without humour. 'Let's just say I've been having persistent fantasies about punching the guy in the face.'

Imogen blinked across at him. 'What are you talking about?'

He gripped his glass, then released it. 'I came to see you, a few nights after we were together. You came off stage and I saw you go to some other man. Hug him, smile at him.'

'That's just Brock,' she said, lifting one shoulder. 'But why would you want to punch him, Luca? You can't seriously have been jealous?'

His smile was cynical. 'Can't I?'

She told herself it meant nothing. A person could absolutely be possessive of another without it suggesting that emotions were involved.

'Of what? You and I hadn't seen each other for three years before that night. We were nothing to each other.'

His frown was contemplative. 'I don't know if that's true.'

She sipped her champagne simply so she had something to do with her hands. 'Then what is true?'

He looked at her without responding, a frown continuing to etch across his face.

'Why did you come to see me?' she persisted, a little breathily.

He arched a brow, as if to imply the answer was obvious.

'Sex?' It flashed in her gut like a flame. She glanced away from him, towards the inky black void where the ocean would be, so she missed the expression that very briefly crossed his face—one of uncertainty. 'Of course, how stupid of me.'

She felt hollowed out and exposed. She was raw and hurt, all over again. She felt that the person she wanted to be with him—strong and unemotional—was far from who she really was. She ground her teeth, trying not to think about her weakness with this man, and how stupid it made her.

'Like I told you, you're a fire in my blood. I didn't think about it. I just knew I had to see you again. Like a moth…'

Her heart raced. Her body trembled. She felt the power of his admission, what it had cost him; she knew how hard that had been. And how much it meant? Could it really mean *anything* when he wasn't prepared to dig deeper and analyse *why* she was a fire in his blood?

'We need to talk,' she said thoughtfully, pausing as his housekeeper brought out a tray of food. Italian delicacies, fresh seafood, *crostini toscani*, *panzanella*. Once she'd left, Imogen leaned a little closer. 'If, and that's a *huge* if, we were to get married, I would need to understand what it would look like.'

He was very still. 'Okay. What would you like to know?'

Heat suffused her cheeks, but she knew she had to get past her embarrassment and be brave. 'Well, where we'd live, and how we'd live—would we share a bedroom or each have our own? Who would get to make the decisions in Aurora's life? For example, who chooses where she goes to school, and who takes her to swimming lessons? Are you going to be hands on with her, or will it go back to being like it was before—with you working from dawn 'til late and us relegated to just the briefest moments in your evening?'

His features tightened and he looked towards the ocean, but when he spoke, his voice was level.

'I presume you'll want to live in London, to be near your family.'

She toyed with the corner of her napkin before reaching for her fork and pressing it into a perfectly seared scampi.

'We're very close,' she admitted.

'That's fine by me. I rarely come to Italy. Though I must admit, seeing Aurora here—'

Imogen's breath caught in her throat. 'I've felt it too.'

Their eyes met and the air between them sparkled.

'It's like she's of this place in some way,' Imogen continued unevenly. 'Seeing her at the beach the other day, it was the strangest sensation of her having come home.'

Luca's jaw shifted, and he made a grunting noise.

'When did you leave Italy?'

'When I was eighteen. As for bedrooms—' he quickly pirouetted the conversation back to their potential marriage '—is there any point in not sharing? We both know how things are between us. Do you want to keep fighting it? Because I sure as hell don't.'

She bit her lip. The problem for Imogen was her inability to separate sex from love. She'd fallen victim to that weakness in the past, and despite everything that lesson had taught her, everything *he'd* taught her, she wasn't sure history wouldn't repeat itself.

'I'll have to think about it,' she responded with caution. 'Why did you leave Italy?'

He looked at her and it was as though she were torturing him, asking him to walk across a bed of nails towards her or something, but he answered, even though the words seemed to have been dredged from his soul against his wishes.

'There was an opportunity in London.'

'No.' She'd had enough of his obfuscation. 'Why did you really leave?'

Again that look of torture. Or terror. 'You know why.'

Yes, she realised, she did. 'You wanted to get away.'

His eyes swept shut.

'Everything here reminds you of your parents, and you were running away from that. You're still running.'

He opened his eyes and lanced her with the directness of his gaze. It was agreement. An admission.

'Luca.' She leaned forward a little, scanning his face, her heart twisting in a way that made her wary, for it indicated in a way that was deeply problematic that his pains were in some way hers. 'I searched you up on the internet, you know. Back then, I mean. There was nothing about your parents, your sister. It was all very bland.'

He nodded once. 'I'm glad.'

'But why isn't there something online? I mean, just a news article, or a mention of you having been orphaned?'

'For the simple reason that I didn't want there to be.'

'That's not really how the internet works.'

His lip quirked in mocking acknowledgement of that. 'After the fire, I went home, and everyone knew about it. Everyone wanted to talk about it, to make sure I was okay. I got tired of pretending I was. My aunt and uncle moved me to a different school, and I began to use their surname. My mother's brother is my uncle, so I didn't see it as a betrayal. Romano is my mother's maiden name.'

'Oh.'

'I couldn't face the constant inquiries. Everywhere I

went, someone brought it up. I wanted to be someone else, someone different. And so, Luca Romano was born.'

'But your aunt and uncle must have wanted to talk to you about it.'

'They wanted to do whatever they could to help me. I just wanted to be left alone.'

Imogen frowned. 'Did you see a therapist, Luca?'

He pulled a face. 'Once. It wasn't helpful.'

A lump formed in her throat. She saw him again as a little boy, a twelve-year-old on the cusp of manhood, grappling with huge emotions and trying to shape them around his ideals of manhood, maturity, masculinity and responsibility.

'Oh, Luca,' she sighed.

'Don't pity me. I don't want it.'

'How can I not pity you? What you went through was awful.'

'It was a long time ago.'

She shook her head. 'But look at how it still affects you.'

'Is there a statute of limitations on grieving your parents, your sister?'

'That's not what I meant.'

'Then what do you mean?'

She bit into her lower lip, food forgotten. 'Grief left unexplored metastasises and forms a hard, hard lump. That lump gets bigger and bigger as time goes on.'

'Speaking from experience?'

She glanced down at her plate, her heart thumping. She couldn't compare her grief to his. She'd been heartbroken, it was true, but that was nothing compared to having lost your parents and sister.

She shook her head slowly. 'I don't know.'

'What is it, *cara*?'

The term of endearment slipped through her, landing dangerously close to her heart. She pushed it aside, assuring herself it was just the way he spoke. Just the way he was sometimes. It didn't mean anything; none of this did. But when she tried to reassure herself that she still hated him, because of how he'd treated her, she found it harder to believe than she had even a week ago.

'Nothing. I'm just saying you need to process what happened, to let yourself off the hook.'

'Why?'

'So you can live without guilt. So you can live at all.'

'I don't want to live.'

She took in a sharp breath.

'Not in the way you mean it. I don't deserve to.'

Her heart trembled. 'How can you say that?' She was aghast, pained.

'Easily. If it weren't for me, they'd still be here. I should have died with them that night. I didn't, but that gives me no pleasure.'

'You really wish you'd died?'

'Of course.'

'No,' she denied hotly, food forgotten as she stood and crossed to him, sitting on his lap and grabbing his cheeks in both hands. 'Don't you dare say that. Your parents would be devastated to know you felt that way.'

A muscle jerked in his jaw. 'It's how I deserve to feel.'

'Luca, stop. You deserve to be here, you deserve to live—and not just to live but to live well.'

'I deserve *niente*. This is not self-pity. I am certainly not looking for your pity. I'm simply stating the facts.'

'As you perceive them, yes,' she agreed quickly, because she could tell there was no artifice to this, no bravado. He felt as he said he did—he felt it to his core—and that dreadful belief had guided his each and every move from when he was a boy. She pressed a kiss to his forehead.

'You survived, and if your parents could tell you anything, it would be that they are glad for that. You said it yourself—you lit up their lives, just by walking in the room. That you are here would mean everything to them.'

He didn't respond. All she could hope was that on some level he'd heard her words, and that he might even let them filter through to his mind, to begin changing his perception of things.

CHAPTER TEN

SHE WAS WRONG. Not about his parents, but about his deserving to let go and live. He couldn't. He had killed his parents, and while he appreciated Imogen's inherently good and kind nature—that she could care about him enough to offer such advice after what he'd done to her—his whole life was, and had been for a long time, predicated on the fact that he had done something so heinous and unforgivable that he would always, always be alone.

The more he wanted someone or something, the more he fought it. The more he thought a path might lead to happiness, the harder he drew back from that path.

Imogen was a perfect case in point.

He wasn't a fool.

He knew that sex had been a cornerstone of what they'd shared, but only because he'd kept it that way. He'd known what the potential had been. He'd known how dangerous it was to be with someone like her, who had obsessed him to the point of distraction.

Every morning, he'd woken up and sworn that would be the last time he saw her, but then he'd always weakened. It had been a never-ending cycle of dependency, until she'd done the one thing that had convinced him it had to end, then and there.

She'd fallen in love with him. Or she'd believed she had, anyway. She'd offered him the one thing he'd known he'd never accept: love. Because to let someone love you was to imply you thought yourself worthy of that love, and for Luca, that would mean forgiving himself on some level. As though his parents' and sister's deaths hadn't meant anything.

And now he had to walk an even finer tightrope. Marriage to Imogen was essential for many reasons. She'd asked what the marriage would look like, and he hadn't been able to give a clear-cut answer. He knew only that he would still need boundaries. Barriers. Roadblocks. Defences.

She had to keep hating him, or at least to never love him again. She needed to stop looking at him with those gentle, perceptive eyes, as if understanding way too much about him.

Because the moment this thing started to feel real, he would need to put distance between them again. He would never let her love him, or even care for him. He would never weaken. He wasn't worthy; he just had to make sure she remembered that.

It was an almost impossible scenario to manage. To marry a woman who was more alluring than any he'd ever known, and to keep her at arm's length, all the while knowing their chemistry would make it impossible not to fall into bed together?

He clenched his teeth, his spine infusing with iron.

It would be difficult, but it had to be done. Not marrying her wasn't an option. It made him too vulnerable, too exposed to the possibility that she'd meet someone else and he'd lose her altogether. That he'd lose Aurora as well. He had to find a way to make it work. Determination flooded his veins; he would do this. He had to.

'Do you see them often?' Imogen curled her legs beneath her on the sofa, a cup of tea clasped in her hands.

He glanced across to her, a frown on his face. 'Who?'

'Your aunt and uncle. Your cousins.'

He was quiet a beat, then shook his head. 'I have only seen them once or twice since I left.'

Imogen's face softened with sympathy. 'You don't get on?'

'I get on with them fine.'

'Then why don't you see them? They're family, Luca.'

Because they loved him. They forgave him. They acted as if it hadn't happened.

'I've been busy.'

She sighed—a soft, husky sound that curled around his chest. 'No one's too busy to see family. Even just for a weekend.'

His grip tightened on his coffee cup. 'We email.'

He practically heard her rolling her eyes. 'That's the same thing.'

'Why does it matter?'

'I don't know yet, but I'm convinced it does. You push people away as a matter of course, even your own flesh and blood.'

'More psychoanalysing?'

'You're the father of my child,' she said softly. 'You're trying to get me to marry you, for her sake. You want to give her a family and I want that too—I do.' She paused, as if weighing her words. 'But what if you decide to push her away, like you did with me? I have to protect her.'

A muscle jerked in his jaw. Imogen was right. He'd

given her no reason to believe he was trustworthy. In fact, he'd demonstrated he wasn't. The fact she was even giving him a chance was, again, a testament to her goodness rather than an indication of him deserving it.

'I won't let her down.'

She sipped her tea.

How could he make her understand?

'I never wanted to have children. I've known that for a long time. That, however, was a theoretical viewpoint. From the moment I realised I was already a dad, that Aurora was here, my child, my daughter—' his voice cracked a little '—I have known the role I would want to play in her life. With Aurora, it's not about me. It's about her. I will spend the rest of my life being whatever she needs me to be.'

Imogen nodded once, blinking away from him. He still wasn't sure if he'd convinced her.

'My aunt and uncle don't need me. They have children. They raised me because they felt they had to, after my parents died. There was no one else to take me in.'

'Luca, how can you say that? They're your family; they love you.'

'No.' He said the word like a curse. 'They don't. Or if they do, they're wrong to.'

Imogen closed her eyes; he had no way of knowing what he was thinking. 'You have to forgive yourself.'

He dismissed her words. She didn't understand. She couldn't. Imogen was too good to properly grasp the depths of his guilt. Silence sparked between them, and when she opened her eyes and pinned him with her gaze, there was a sadness in her expression that washed over him, leaving his chest heavy and sore.

'Poor Luca,' she sighed, reaching across and putting

a hand on his, briefly. He refused to allow the gesture to comfort him, even when her touch pulled at something in his gut, as it always did. When he didn't say anything in response, she stood, removing her hand. Coldness settled around him.

'I think I'll go for a walk.' She gestured towards the garden. 'I…want to soak all this in, before we leave.'

She walked away and he expelled a long, slow breath of relief. For reasons beyond his comprehension, he was telling Imogen things that he had never contemplated sharing with another soul. He was opening up to her in a way that was anathema to him. Because of the stakes now? Because he had to convince her he could be trusted in marriage? Of course. She was smart and she was cautious, with good reason. Showing her his mentality would serve two purposes: she would understand that when it came to his daughter, he would do everything he could to live up to his father's example; and it would also serve as an insurance policy against her ever believing herself in love with him again.

Imogen walked, and she thought, and the more she did so, the more confused and sad she became. The more she wanted to make excuses for him and the more she ached for him, the more she realised that they were in a very difficult situation.

And protecting her heart seemed at once both vitally important and impossible.

It was strange to miss a place having only spent a few days there, but arriving back in London, Imogen had to admit that she had a hankering to be in the sunlit Tuscan countryside, or at the delightful white sand cove, rather than in the city that was gradually turning grey and cool as autumn took a real hold.

The impulse to run away was natural, Imogen knew. She'd felt it herself, after Luca had dumped her, and when she'd discovered she was pregnant. But she had strong, deep-rooted connections to a supportive and loving family.

And in time, the feelings had lessened, the sting of hurt had faded—even when it'd left in its wake a certainty that she'd never be the same again.

Six years had elapsed between Luca's tragedy and his leaving Italy. Six years in which she imagined that poor young boy had been running from his grief the whole time. Even before he'd left the country, he'd changed his name and school, changed everything that had linked him to his immediate family and that accident.

He'd been running for longer than he hadn't been. It was a habit now, as worn into him as was breathing and walking.

He'd never stop running and she needed to accept that, or she'd get hurt all over again.

The idea of keeping a distance from him was becoming harder and harder. She was a human being, not an automaton, and there was something about Luca that just got under her skin.

But as he'd said, this wasn't about them. It wasn't about him; it wasn't about her. They were parents, and they both wanted to give Aurora the same kind of loving childhood they'd benefited from. Perhaps that was even more important to Luca, because of how his world had been so drastically and awfully shattered. Aurora deserved the best of them; she always would. And Imogen was starting to realise that Luca was right: they could give that to her, so long as they worked together.

She found him in his bedroom, tightening a tie around his neck, and for a moment it was impossible to speak because he was so strikingly handsome, her whole world tilted on its edge.

'This won't be easy, and it won't be simple, but okay,' she said, slowly, giving herself every chance to back out even then.

He turned to face her, and it was obvious he understood what she was referring to despite the lack of preamble. 'You're sure?'

She laughed softly, shaking her head. 'Not really. But I know we won't regret trying this. For Aurora's sake.'

He stalked across the carpet to her, taking her hands in his and lifting them to his lips. 'For Aurora,' he agreed, but when he kissed her, it definitely didn't feel that it was about anyone but them, Imogen and Luca, with a fever in both their bloods and a need time seemed unable to extinguish.

He pulled away though, looking down at her, his face so close she could see every fleck of gold in his eyes, each dark, clearly defined lash that circled them. She could see the turmoil there, the thoughts.

'You're not happy,' she murmured, then could have kicked herself. Of course he wasn't happy. This wasn't a normal engagement. She wasn't making all his dreams come true by agreeing to become his wife.

'I'm relieved,' he admitted, and her chest panged a little. 'But, Imogen—' He broke off, frowning deeply. 'You were hurt by me in the past. I don't want to hurt you again. It's important that we both go into this with our eyes open.'

'My eyes are open,' she said quietly.

'If I was a different man—' his voice was gruff '—you would be all my dreams come true.'

Her heart churned.

'But I'm not. This is who I am, who I'll always be. I don't want marrying me to be a ticket to misery for you.'

'Three years ago, I didn't understand. I thought we were something we weren't. I thought you wanted the same thing as me.'

'That was my fault.'

She bit into her lip. She couldn't deny that. 'I didn't have enough experience to see what you were clearly trying to show me. I took everything about you at face value—I presumed your having to go to the office early to be about your workload, rather than you putting a ring-fence around the time we would spend together.'

His skin paled slightly, and his lips tightened. 'I should never have been with you.' He wiped a thumb over her lower lip, and his voice was rich with earnest pain. 'You trusted me, but I was never worthy of that trust.'

For three years she'd been desperate for him to apologise. To hear him say how wrong he'd been, to say he regretted it. But those words gave her little satisfaction now.

'I should have walked away after that first night, but you were so—'

'So?'

He shook his head slowly. 'I don't know.' The answer was honest, if frustrating. 'There was something about you, about how I felt when I was with you.'

Her stomach churned.

'I should have known better then, and I want to do better now.'

'We will.'

He squeezed her hands. 'I wish I could offer you more.'

Something like grief washed over her.

'You deserve more.'

She shook her head, denying it without understanding. 'Are you trying to talk me out of marrying you now?' she half joked.

'No. I still want this. I just need to know you're sure.'

She sucked in a deep breath. 'I'm not sure about everything,' she said after a beat. 'I'm not sure how it will work, I'm not sure that it's not a mistake, but I'm sure I want to try. I'm sure we both have the stubbornness and determination to make it work. So, let's do it.'

His face relaxed a little, and he nodded. 'Okay then. Let's get married.'

Her heart popped in a way that made Imogen realise it didn't understand. This was just an arrangement. It wasn't real at all.

Telling Genevieve was not something Imogen was looking forward to, and it was certainly not something she wanted to do with Luca in the house. So, she waited until he was at work, then invited Genevieve over for lunch. She made a simple soup and fed Aurora early, so she was ready for a nap by the time Genevieve arrived.

Aurora's aunt gave her a cuddle and insisted on settling her to bed, then came into the kitchen, where Imogen was spooning lunch into two bowls and removing crusty garlic bread from the oven.

'God, I miss her,' Genevieve murmured as she walked into the state-of-the-art kitchen. 'Please tell me you're coming home soon? It's so depressing without you guys.'

Imogen's stomach was in knots. This was the moment of truth. 'Actually, Gen, I need to tell you something.' She passed one bowl of soup towards her sister before taking a seat at the kitchen bench. She made no attempt to reach for her own bowl. She was far too anxious.

'What?' But Genevieve's hesitation was telling. She knew something was going on. 'Im?'

'Luca asked me to marry him.'

Genevieve closed her eyes. 'And you told him to go to hell, right?'

Imogen bit down on her lip. 'At first.'

'Oh, God.'

'Hear me out.'

Genevieve blinked across at her sister, shaking her head. 'I've heard you out, though. I heard you crying, Im. Every night, for months on end. I watched you grow thin and pale, even though you were pregnant. I watched you stare into space, your face tormented by memories you wouldn't share. I saw you fall apart at the seams because of that bastard, and now you're going back to him?'

'It's not like that,' Imogen whispered, her voice cracking a little. 'This isn't the same as before.'

'Really? Because it sounds a bit the same.'

'I know him so much better now. I understand him.'

'If that were true, you'd be running a mile.'

'Gen, I love you to bits, and I know you're trying to be supportive of me. But you *don't* know him.'

'I've known men like him, and I know what he did to you before. Leopards don't change their spots.'

'He's not changing his spots—I just see them better now.'

'What does that even mean?'

'We're not in love. This isn't about us. It's about giving Aurora the kind of family that matters to both of us.'

Genevieve stared at Imogen as though she'd gone mad. 'Are you hearing yourself?'

'I know, I know. It's not…like me,' she said with a lift of one shoulder. 'But some things matter more than romance and being swept off your feet. I want to do this for Aurora. I want her to have what we had growing up.'

'But you guys aren't Mum and Dad. You just said it yourself—you don't love each other. Kids are perceptive. She's going to see that her parents hate each other—'

'We don't hate each other either.'

'You have hated him for three years. I've heard the songs.'

Imogen winced a little, thinking of the enormous catalogue of songs she'd written, most of them inspired by the feelings he'd caused her to have.

'That was then.'

'But what's functionally changed? You always knew he was Aurora's father.'

'I've seen another side to him.'

Genevieve pulled a sceptical face.

'Gen, I'm going into this with my eyes wide open.'

'That's no guarantee your heart won't get broken.'

'But my heart has nothing to do with this. We're getting married for Aurora.'

'So there's nothing going on between the two of you? You're not sleeping with him?'

Imogen glanced down at her soup, her cheeks flushing pink.

'You're not going to bed together and waking up finding it hard to clutch at the threads of reality because in that moment, you're side by side and he's everything you want in life?'

Imogen gasped.

'I'm your twin,' Genevieve muttered.

'Yeah, well, you're not psychic. I don't feel like that,' Imogen denied hotly.

'You can lie to me, but please don't lie to yourself.'

'I'm not.'

'You're not capable of being in a relationship with someone and not loving them.'

Imogen gasped. 'Why do I feel like that's an insult?'

'It's not, believe me. It's one of the things that's different about you and me. You give with all of yourself. You can't help it. You're the same with friends, family, Aurora. You put all of your heart into the people you're with, and if that's him, then you're going to do the same. Except he will chew you up and spit you out for breakfast.'

'Don't say that,' Imogen whispered, her heart dropping to her toes. Was Genevieve right? She'd spent so much time with Luca since coming to live with him. Was it possible he'd brainwashed her, and she just wasn't seeing the forest for the trees?

'Listen, Imogen. I want you to be happy. You're my sister, and I love you. But I'll have no part in this sham of a wedding. Get married or don't, but whatever you do, don't expect me to be there on the day. I have no interest in watching you make the biggest mistake of your life, and I'm pretty sure Mum and Dad will feel the same way.'

She stood up, pressed a kiss to Imogen's cheek and then walked towards the kitchen door, soup totally abandoned. 'Oh, and get a damned good prenup, because after he screws you and breaks your heart all over again, you should at least get some of this.' She waved her hand around his expensive town house before blowing a kiss and stalking towards the front door.

Imogen stared at the empty space her twin had previously occupied, her heart thumping hard against her ribs, acid rising in her throat.

Was Genevieve right? Was Imogen about to make the biggest mistake of her life?

Uncertainty settled around her and refused to budge, so by the time Luca returned, she almost couldn't bear to see him.

Unlike in the past, he came home around four, so he was available to spend time with Aurora before she went to bed. He'd become a very involved father, and loved reading to her and running her bath, supervising her dinner, cleaning up afterwards. If Imogen had expected him to want to hire a team of nannies and wash his hands of any actual parenting, she'd been completely mistaken.

When he walked in the door that particular afternoon, Imogen was dressed in her exercise gear. 'I thought I'd go for a run,' she said, not quite meeting his eyes.

He opened his mouth to say something, then closed it and nodded instead. 'Good day?'

'Sure, great day. See you.' She waved in his general direction, opened the door and stepped outside, exhaling into the cool air, grateful to have avoided being face to face to him.

She turned the music up loud on her phone and plugged her ears with earbuds, running hard and fast, doing everything she could to drown out her thoughts. They had been swirling around and around in her mind all day and she needed to escape them.

But she couldn't. Each step made her body tired, but her mind wouldn't stop.

She remembered the time they'd spent together in the past. Each night, each morning, each small little thing. She remembered how easily she'd fallen for him, and how little he'd cared. She remembered their madness in coming together again; she remembered the nights now, the way he was with Aurora, and panic rose inside of her, because they had to get this right, and she had no idea if this was going to be a huge mistake that she'd always regret. What if she was messing everything up for their daughter?

What if she wasn't being honest with herself and she did actually love him? What if, what if, what if?

Frustration was a beast inside of her, uncertainty a wave she couldn't escape.

It was dark by the time she came home, and Aurora was dressed in her pyjamas, reading a book with Luca. Imogen smiled tightly at them both.

'All good?' she asked, moving past them without waiting for an answer.

'*Sì. Perfetto.* And you?'

She nodded quickly. 'I'm going to shower.'

She took her time there, too, hiding out, avoiding him, her brain ticking over, looking at this from every angle. But it didn't matter how many times she pulled at the threads of this—she always came back to the same answer.

They were different now. They were doing this for Aurora, walking into the marriage with their eyes open to the kind of marriage it would be. Imogen wasn't the same girl she'd been back then. It was natural for Genevieve to worry: she'd seen Imogen at her very rock bottom. But so much had changed since then.

They could do this, and it would be fine. It had to be.

CHAPTER ELEVEN

'I'VE BEEN THINKING about the wedding,' she said later that night, as he stacked their plates in the dishwasher.

He turned to face her, giving her his full attention. 'Yes?'

She made a throaty sound of agreement. 'I don't want a big fuss. Why don't we just elope?'

A frown pulled at his lips. 'What about your family? You're close to them. Won't they want to be there?'

She glanced down, hoping he didn't see the hurt in her eyes. The thought of getting married without Genevieve or her parents was awful, but Gen had been right: she couldn't ask them to be a part of something that was so outside the bounds of the kind of marriage they'd want for her. They'd proudly come and watch her get married for love, but not for these reasons.

Though wasn't this a little about love? Love for the child they'd made, love for the little girl who was their whole world? What wouldn't they do, as parents, to secure Aurora's future, to give her everything she deserved in life?

'Imogen? Did something happen today?'

She glanced at him quickly, then away again. 'Why do you ask?'

'You're avoiding me.'

'We just had dinner together.'

'And you were somewhere else the whole time.'

Her stomach squished. He knew her so well; he always had. He could read her like a book.

She blinked quickly. 'I told my sister today. It didn't go well.'

He nodded slowly. 'I see. And that's important to you.'

'She's my sister,' Imogen said, as though that explained it. 'My *twin* sister. We have done everything together for as long as I can remember. She's my biggest cheerleader, my best friend—as I am hers.'

'And she doesn't support the idea of this marriage.'

Imogen shook her head.

'Okay.' He didn't sound deterred. 'Then what would you like to do?'

'I told you, elope.'

'This doesn't make you question what we're doing?'

She shook her head. 'It did. I have been questioning it all afternoon, but I keep coming back to the same conclusion. This is what's right for us. That's not up to anyone else to decide.' She sighed softly. 'What does it matter? This isn't a normal marriage, we don't need anything big. We're just getting married for Aurora, right? So let's elope and be done with it.'

He studied her for a long time, his eyes narrowing, his brow furrowing. 'We can elope, *cara*. Whatever you want is fine by me.'

The next morning, he left as if going to the office, careful to act as though everything was normal. Instead of heading to the City, however, he had his driver take him to a little apartment in Putney. He pressed the doorbell, waited, and when Genevieve opened the door, he braced himself for this conversation.

He'd convinced Imogen this was the right thing to do, but he suspected it was going to be a lot harder winning her sister over. However, having seen the crestfallen look on Imogen's face, the tightness around her eyes, he knew it wasn't optional. Having her twin sister's support really mattered to Imogen, and if he could fix it, then he would.

If not, they'd elope, just the three of them, but he knew that wasn't what Imogen wanted. What she deserved. He was better not thinking about what she deserved, because the second he pulled at that thread, this whole preposterous house of cards fell over.

'You.' Genevieve's voice was a growl.

'Can we talk?'

It was obvious that she wanted to refuse, but at the same time, she loved her sister, and her invitation for him to come into the apartment was clearly motivated by that. 'I've got an appointment, but I can spare five minutes. What do you want?'

'To talk about the wedding.'

Genevieve made a scoffing noise. 'You mean your idea of the century?'

'With respect, your sister is an intelligent woman who's made her own mind up about marrying me.'

'Yeah, she also made her mind up about falling into bed with you three years ago, and again now, and neither of those were particularly strong decisions.'

'You presume to know a lot about our relationship, given you've met me twice.'

'I don't need to know you to know what you're capable of.'

He bristled. Her anger was grating but it was also gratifying. She was speaking to him as he believed he deserved to be spoken to. She viewed him as the worst of the worst and in this way, they were in agreement.

'I'm not going to hurt her.'

She made a noise of disbelief. 'Of course you are.'

'Why do you say that?'

'It's what you do.'

He flinched. Had Imogen told her about his family?

'You hurt her back then, and you're going to hurt her again. I don't know when and I don't know how, but you don't have what it takes to be a decent human and take care of her.'

He flinched again. Every single one of his worst fears was in her words.

'You're not a decent human being.'

'What happened between us in the past was regrettable—'

'Regrettable? You almost killed her. Do you have any idea what it was like for her?'

He blanched. He knew he'd hurt her, but at the same time, she'd downplayed that. She'd told him she'd been fine, that she'd moved on. Or had he simply presumed that, because of the air she projected. She'd told him she hadn't actually loved him.

'If she hadn't been pregnant, I have no idea what would have happened. You *destroyed* my beautiful, loving, free-spirited, kind sister once and I'll be damned if I'm going to let you do it again.'

'Imogen is fine,' he said again, because he needed to believe that was true. 'She was fine—'

'You didn't just break her heart—you broke her soul, her spirit, her everything. You are a monster and I will always hate you.'

Just like Imogen had promised. Did a part of her still hate him?

'She told me it wasn't a big deal,' he said, searching for something to grab hold of.

'She lied. Probably to protect her pride or maybe even to protect you, because she's just that much of a good-hearted fool, apparently.'

He shook his head. 'She's not a fool.' But hadn't she been the definition of that three years ago? She'd kept coming to him, wanting him, needing him, when he hadn't deserved her. Anyone could have seen that, but Imogen had been his regardless.

He dropped his head forward, stars in his eyes as the full impact of his carelessness three years ago came home to roost.

'We both know what she was back then,' Genevieve ground out. 'Imogen was innocent, totally inexperienced. And do you know why?'

'No.' He'd never bothered to ask. He hadn't under-stood it, but she'd acted like it was no big deal, and he'd accepted that at face value. Because he hadn't wanted to dig deeper? He hadn't been willing to hear that it had been something she'd been saving?

'She didn't fool around in college like the rest of us. She went on a couple of dates, here and there, but she always kept a level head because she was waiting to meet "the one."'

His skin paled beneath his tan.

'The first night she met you, she came home on cloud nine. She was in love even then.'

'That's not true.'

Genevieve rolled her eyes. 'If you're going to marry her, you need to know the full story. You think she's strong and brave? Well, she is, but not where you're concerned. You have to be strong and brave for her, and save her from making the same mistake all over again.'

Hadn't he been trying to do that? He'd been honest with her all along, making sure she understood his boundaries this time. Hell, he'd even explained why he was this way.

But hadn't he also been selfish? If he really cared about protecting her, he wouldn't be sleeping with her every chance he got. He'd be working out a way to co-parent that was respectful, amicable, and had zero risk to Imogen.

There was also the possibility, though, of her meeting someone else, and when he thought of that, it was like the air had been sucked from his lungs. He couldn't breathe; he could barely stand. That wasn't a good enough reason to tie her up in this marriage, though.

Only, Imogen had assured him, again and again, that she wanted this. That she was okay. That she understood his boundaries. What right did he or Genevieve have to question that?

'This isn't your decision.'

'But it is yours.'

'No, it's Imogen's.'

'And you're really happy to let her make this mistake again?'

'What mistake? We are marrying to give our daughter a family. This matters to us both.'

'That might be why you're marrying her, but I can guarantee it's more than that for Imogen. She probably doesn't even realise that yet, but if you think she doesn't love you, you're an idiot.'

He stared at her. 'She does not love me.' She couldn't. No one could. Memories of that morning, with the sunlight shifting through the bedroom window, as Imogen had rolled over and told him she loved him, slammed into him, unwanted and awful—memories he rarely examined because the feelings had been too extreme to navigate.

'I'm as shocked as you are,' Genevieve muttered.

'Three years ago, we misunderstood one another—'

Genevieve made a noise and rolled her eyes. 'Whatever.'

He frowned. 'She has told me she didn't love me. That she only thought she did, because of her inexperience. We've both moved on.'

Genevieve looked at him, aghast, then shook her head. 'Wait here a second.'

She returned a moment later with a CD.

'Listen to her music. She might have told you something, just like she might have told me something, but in her music, she's always honest. Go, listen to the songs, then tell me this is a risk you're happy to take. Tell me you're not going to mess her up all over again.'

He played the CD on the drive to his office, but even when the car pulled into the secure car park, he continued to sit where he was, listening to each and every lyric, his heart pounding so hard and fast it formed a new backing track to the songs.

These were incredible songs. Songs of desperation. Of love. Of yearning and need. Of hurt and anger and hatred. In these eight songs, he ran the full gamut of her feelings, from realising she loved him, to her breaking heart, to her utter dejection and misery, the feeling of betrayal and then angry hatred. He recognised the last song. It had been a huge hit, played everywhere in the world when it was first released and for months afterwards. It must have been the song she'd told him of, the song that had been purchased off this demo.

He groaned, dropping his head into his hands. She'd sung this song at the bar, and looked at him—how good that must have felt for her, to be able to serenade him with a hate song she'd written just for him.

He dragged his hands through his hair, the world tipping wildly onto its side. Because Genevieve was right, and he'd known it all along. The album gave him more of an understanding and insight, but it was just clarifying something he'd been feeling, instincts he'd been having, since she'd first come back into his life.

He was playing with fire, and didn't he know the reality of that? Fire always burned. Fire killed.

No way would he put Imogen through this again. No way on earth, no way in hell. He cared for her. Recognising that was like the slipping into place of a foundational brick. He *cared* for her. He'd cared for her then too. That was why he'd reacted so harshly, needed to break things off swiftly, to make her hate him. And he cared for her now, too much to let her be hurt. He cared for her enough to set her free.

With Aurora settled in bed for the night, Imogen pulled a lasagne from the oven and began to serve their dinner, but Luca forestalled her. 'Do you mind if we talk a minute?'

She frowned. 'Can we talk over dinner? I'm starving.'

He frowned. 'Sure, okay.'

She glanced at him. 'Is everything all right?'

'Fine.' His smile was forced though, and a sense of uncertainty spread through her. Nonetheless, she served up their lasagne, handing a plate to him. But he collected both and carried them through to the dining table, which she'd set earlier with placemats and cutlery.

'What did you want to talk about?'

He looked down at her lasagne. 'Eat first.'

She took a scoop of the food to her mouth, enjoyed the flavours, but was impatient to know what was on his mind. He was adamant, though, and waited until she'd almost finished before leaning back in his chair a little, his own meal untouched.

'I made a mistake, Imogen.' His words were wooden. She glanced at him, not sure what he meant.

'What with?'

'Us. This.'

She was very still. 'I beg your pardon?'

'The marriage. It's a mistake. I didn't think it through.'

She pressed her cutlery to the table, appetite completely gone. 'What?'

'We can be in Aurora's life without marrying. We can even live together. But I think it's imperative that the lines not be blurred between us—as a man and woman, and as parents.'

The blood in her veins turned to ice. 'What does that mean?'

His lips compressed. 'We're attracted to each other. We always have been. But the moment I knew about Aurora, that should have been the end of it. Sex between us is a mistake. Getting married is a mistake. We will do better by Aurora if we find a way to work together that doesn't have the potential to blow up in our faces.'

'I thought that's what we were doing.'

A muscle throbbed in his jaw. 'Three years ago, I ruined your life. I'm not going to do it again.'

'You didn't ruin my life,' she denied, clinging to that falsehood. 'I was fine.'

'You were not fine.' His back was ramrod straight. 'I heard the songs.'

She blinked quickly. 'You what?'

'I heard the songs.'

'How could you—' She closed her eyes as comprehension dawned. 'Genevieve.'

He dipped his head once. 'She was looking out for your best interests—as I should have done.'

'Damn it.' Imogen slammed her palm against the table. 'Did it occur to either of you that I'm a big girl who can look after my *own* interests?'

'Like you did three years ago?'

'I'm not the same person any more.'

'And why not?'

She went silent.

'You're not that same beautiful, innocent, trusting woman because I broke you.' His voice was rent with self-directed anger. 'I destroyed you. I heard the lyrics. Every single word was written for me, about me, about us, about what I did to you. I will not take that risk again.'

'I was fine,' she repeated, aware they both knew it was a lie.

He shook his head once, seeing through it. 'This was a mistake.'

'How come I don't get to decide that?'

'Because you're too damned good,' he muttered. 'You're not the same as you were three years ago, but you're still too fair-minded, too kind. You would marry me because of Aurora, and you'll look past any of my faults because of what I've been through. You put everyone ahead of yourself and it has to stop.'

She gawped, his words etching lines in her soul. 'What if this marriage is what I want?'

He ground his teeth. 'We both know it's not.'

Imogen jammed her lips together, on the brink of saying something she knew she'd regret. Because he was wrong. This marriage had come to mean so much more to her. It wasn't just about Aurora, or the past. It was the slotting into place of a piece of her that she hadn't realised she'd been missing.

She toyed with her fork, trying not to react as her mind spun faster and faster.

The truth was, Luca was a part of her.

He always had been.

Not all of him—he would never give all of himself to anyone. But that didn't matter. Imogen would take the bread crumbs. Just as she had back then.

Because she loved him.

She sucked in a soft breath, the thought almost knocking her sideways.

She loved him now, just as much as she had then. No—more. She loved him because she knew him so much better now. She understood his faults and flaws and the reason for them. She understood the trauma he'd survived but found it impossible to live through, a trauma that had trapped him in an awful, awful web of misery and self-loathing. A trauma that had made him sabotage any relationship, push everyone away, even his aunt and uncle and especially Imogen.

He was doing it again now. He was making it seem as if it was about protecting her, but that wasn't true. At least, it wasn't the whole truth. He was protecting himself. Because he loved her? The suspicion popped into her mind unbidden and, at first, she yearned to dismiss it.

Why would she be stupid enough to believe he loved her? What kind of glutton for punishment was she?

And yet, didn't it make sense?

He had been a lone wolf for so long, and completely by choice, because he wouldn't let himself be loved; he didn't think he was worthy of it. Could it be true? Her heart hurt at the very idea.

'What do *you* want, Luca?'

'That's not important.'

'Says who?'

'Me.' His lips curved into a mocking smile. 'Your sister.'

'Ignore Gen, for now.'

'I can't. She knows you better than anyone.'

'Does she?' Imogen challenged. 'You don't think you know me pretty well by now, too?'

'I didn't know about this.'

Imogen's cheeks flushed pink. 'I'm a musician,' she muttered dismissively. 'Writing about my feelings is a part of what I do. Sometimes it sounds worse than it is.'

'I don't believe you.'

She didn't contradict him. Her songs were an accurate reflection of how she'd felt at the time. 'Okay,' she said unevenly. 'You broke me. You did. I fell in love with you—I don't mean I thought I loved you. I fell in actual, hard, all-consuming love with you and then you talked to me as if I was nothing. Nobody. Like I could walk out of your house, and you wouldn't ever think of me again. Do you have any idea how tortured I was by the idea of you and other women? You said you'd replace me straightaway, and all I could think about, night after night after night, was you doing exactly that.'

He sat completely still, his face a mask of impenetrable cool, but she could see the emotions in his eyes and knew he was feeling this. She knew he was hurting too.

'I should never have said that. I just needed you to leave.'

'You were honest with me.' She tilted her chin. 'And even though it hurt, I'm glad. You were honest with me that day and you've been honest with me ever since. No matter what happens, you have never promised me something you couldn't give me.'

'That's not true.' His voice was gravelled. 'I promised I wouldn't hurt you, but I'm not so sure about that now.'

'Again, that's not up to you.'

He shook his head. 'You're misunderstanding me. This isn't a debate. I'm not marrying you, Imogen. I won't do it to either of us.'

Her lips parted on a soft breath, surprise contorting her features. 'I can't believe this.' She pushed back from the table and stood, her whole body shaking. 'So what do you want, Luca?'

He stared at her for several seconds. 'I want to work out how to do this without messing everything up. We're Aurora's parents, but that's where it has to end. We can parent together, be civil to one another, but we can no longer sleep together, or eat meals together as if something more is going to come of this. I know it won't, and going through the motions feels a hell of a lot like leading you on.'

She stared at him, her heart pounding against her ribs. He was right. He hadn't led her on, but everything they'd been doing had become real to her, despite his warnings, his insistence on maintaining boundaries. Even in spite of her own certainty that she would be able to keep this in a box this time around. She hadn't. She couldn't.

She dropped her head, the reality spilling over into her soul. 'I need to think,' she muttered, stalking towards the door, slipping her feet into shoes and leaving the house before she screamed. She was so damned angry, so frustrated, she wanted to punch something. Instead, she slammed the door behind her, then slumped her shoulders and let a single tear roll down her cheek.

How could she be here again?

CHAPTER TWELVE

HE'D DONE THE right thing. He'd hated every minute of it, but wasn't that the point? He was back in his comfort zone, back where he thrived.

Alone.

Angry at the world.

Angry with himself.

He paced the living room like a caged beast, each stride a commitment to this path. Imogen couldn't become collateral damage in his quest for misery. Imogen had to be set free.

He had done the right thing.

He repeated it, as a mantra, because in saying it, the words became something solid to cling to, a reassurance in a sea of uncertainty, an unravelling of all that he'd held fast to all his adult life.

'I thought I'd see you,' Genevieve said, opening the door to their flat and waving Imogen inside.

Imogen shook her head at her sister, angry, sad, bereft. 'You had no business getting involved, Gen.'

'You think? Who picked up the pieces last time? Literally held the baby while you were coping with what he did to you?'

'All he did to me was not love me back. That's not a crime, and it's not something you need to punish him for.'

'No,' she agreed. 'But you're planning to marry the guy, so of course he should fully comprehend what that means for you.'

'Don't you think that's my decision?'

'When it comes to Luca Romano, you make terrible decisions.'

Imogen ground her teeth together. 'Luca is—' She shook her head. 'You don't know him.'

'I know that he's going to marry you, even though I've told him how disastrous it will be for you. I know that he's a selfish son of—'

'No,' Imogen spat, shaking her head as tears stung her lashes. 'He's not.'

Silence crackled between the sisters.

'He's called it off.'

Genevieve let out a low whistle, moving towards Imogen and wrapping her in a hug. The floodgates opened then, and Imogen sobbed against her.

'Oh, honey,' Genevieve murmured. 'I know it doesn't feel like it right now, but it's for the best.'

'It feels like the opposite of that,' she whispered. 'I understand why you're worried, but Gen, I'm telling you, Luca is… There's something about him. He's…'

'He's Aurora's father,' Genevieve said. 'Of course you feel something for him. You'll always share her, and—'

'No, this is about him and me. We're like magnets. No—' She pulled back as realisation dawned. 'We're like soulmates,' she corrected. 'My soul seeks his soul and nothing else matters.'

'Do you hear yourself?' Genevieve groaned. 'How can you say that after what he did to you?'

'You don't understand. He is on a path of self-sabotage. He refuses to get close to anyone. He's been fighting me this whole time, but that doesn't mean he doesn't want this. In fact, the harder he fights, the more he wants. I know it sounds ridiculous—'

'Yeah. It really does. If someone loves you, they say that. They put it out in the open because nothing is simpler or more important than love. Luca doesn't love you.'

'Then why call off the wedding?' Imogen challenged. 'If he doesn't care about me, why not just marry me, to hell with the consequences for me?'

'Because he's not a total jerk,' Genevieve conceded. 'He must have some scruples, somewhere in that big, dumb head of his.'

Imogen stiffened, pulled back from her sister. 'I know you think I'm doing the wrong thing—'

'I *know* it, with all my heart.'

'Okay.' Imogen blinked slowly. She loved her sister; they were closer than the best of friends. But Imogen still had to live her life and make her choices. 'I'm sorry you feel that way, I really am.'

'But you're going to marry him anyway.'

'If I can change his mind, yes. I'm going to marry him.'

And for the first time in days, she felt the certainty of that decision like a blade in her spine, a strengthening force that had her standing tall, staring right into her future. Every single piece of her was pushing her towards this, and him.

For the smallest window of time, he'd let this feel real. He'd let it feel real even when that broke every rule he'd set for himself. And he'd been telling himself it was all in his control, that they were on the same page. He'd told himself she wouldn't get hurt because he kept laying out the ground rules, but he hadn't really understood just how explosive things were between them. Trying to control this situation was like trying to tame the ocean.

He should have ended things between them the moment he'd found out about Aurora.

He paced the lounge room, listening to small noises from upstairs—Imogen singing to their daughter, speaking softly. Reading, perhaps. When she came down, they'd finish the conversation he'd started the night before and begin drawing up a future that didn't involve a personal relationship.

It would serve him right. Not just for what he did to his own family, but for how he'd treated Imogen. He would be a spectator in her life for ever, watching her go from strength to strength—as surely she must. He no longer feared her meeting someone else. He almost relished the prospect. Let him stand by and watch her be swept off her feet, as she deserved. Let him watch her be joyously happy with a man who wasn't broken and damaged, who was capable of loving her as she deserved. Let that man form the family Imogen wanted and Aurora deserved.

His gut twisted and seemed to drop to his toes; the pain of that spectre almost weakened his resolve, so he ran his palm across his scarred chest, the ridges palpable through the cotton of his shirt, reminding him of the core beliefs that had defined his life.

He'd given up so much in the name of punishment; this was just one more sacrifice.

'She's asleep.' Imogen's voice was soft, tentative. As if she knew they had a messy conversation ahead of them and was bracing herself for it.

'Good.' He turned to face her, felt his stomach tighten

at the sight of her, the way her long hair was loose and wavy around her face, tousled like it became after they made love. He looked away quickly, jaw clenched. 'Are you hungry?'

'No.'

When he glanced back at her, Imogen had wrapped her hands around her waist, as if to offer herself comfort. He cursed inwardly; he had to stop hurting her. He had to get her out of his orbit, in which everything he touched turned to dust.

'I spoke to a lawyer today.'

Imogen's sharp intake of breath shouldn't have surprised him. She was afraid he was going to take away their daughter, even now? One look at her face confirmed that—she was paler than a ghost.

'To discuss how to set up a shared custody arrangement,' he continued, his voice eerily calm given the maelstrom of his emotions. 'Since learning about Aurora, I have made a mistake at almost every opportunity. It's time to start getting things right.'

Imogen's lips parted, but a little colour returned to her face. 'You acted out of love—'

He opened his mouth to deny it, but as if she couldn't bear to hear that denial, Imogen quickly continued.

'For our daughter. Every decision you made was borne of a love for her, right?'

He ground his teeth. 'Please, don't do that.'

'Don't do what?'

'Make excuses for me.'

'Is that what I'm doing?'

'It stops you from seeing me as I really am.'

'I've been seeing you this whole time, Luca. Way better than you see yourself.'

'No.' The word was rich with finality, a sharp denial. 'I'm not going to get into this with you. We're not discussing me, or my merits. There's no point. Let's keep things relevant to Aurora.'

She opened her mouth and then sighed, shaking her head a little before moving with innate grace towards one of the armchairs. She didn't sit down, though; instead, Imogen pressed her hands to the back of it, using it almost as a shield.

'What did the lawyer say?'

'There are several options, depending on what we think will work best. One solution is nest parenting,' he said, voice gruff. 'We have a shared home, which is for Aurora, and we move in and out. I stay with her, then you do, and vice versa, so she continues to have a stable residence. The lawyer said this may be particularly helpful to school-aged children, who have busy schedules and would prefer not to be lugging things from one parent's house to another.'

Imogen's eyes were wet with unshed tears; she didn't bother to blink them away.

Seeing them only hardened his resolve.

This was what he did. *This* was what he was good at, and why he had to let her go. If she stayed with him, he would keep hurting her, even when he didn't want to.

'Alternatively, we can stick to a more standard custody arrangement, where I have Aurora here some of the time and you have her the rest.' He frowned, a deep groove. 'However, I would insist on buying you a home, ideally somewhere near mine. Naturally, your sister could live with you there.'

Imogen blinked rapidly. 'I have a home.'

'You have a flat,' he responded sharply, then softened

his tone. He hated everything about this conversation, though, and it was impossible to keep that from his voice and manner. 'Aurora will need more space as she gets older, she'll need more things. And vitally, I would like her to know that I am looking after her mother.'

Imogen bristled. 'I don't need you to look after me.'

He felt the hint of combat in her voice and tried to calm his own rioting emotions. 'I mean to financially support you, as I would have been doing all along, had I known about her.'

Imogen dropped her head forward, staring at the back of the armchair as though it was endlessly fascinating to her.

'The lawyer said that given our relative financial positions, a support arrangement would form part of a shared parenting agreement.'

'Please, stop.' She whispered the words, but they seemed to reverberate around the house as if she'd yelled them. 'Don't say another word.'

Per her request, he compressed his lips, crossing his arms over her chest. Silence now rebounded against the walls, bouncing in a way that he felt in the core of his being.

Imogen lifted her head slowly, and for a moment, accusation glittered in her eyes before it was replaced by something else. Determination? Impatience?

'You and I agreed to get married because we wanted to give Aurora the kind of family life that we both enjoyed, a family life that matters to us. We wanted her mother and father living together, under one roof, supporting her, loving her, building her up before she goes out into the world on her own. *You're* the one who has been pushing that all along, and I don't think it's fair that you get to just pull that away from me when you decide to.'

Waves of emotion rolled through him. Fair? *Fair?* What about this was fair? What about *anything* in life was?

He slashed a frustrated hand through the air. 'We cannot separate us as people from us as parents.'

Imogen made a scoffing noise. 'Isn't that normal?'

'Not for us. Not for what we are.'

'You keep trying to define us. Why can't you just let us be, and see where this goes?'

'We've done that,' he responded sharply. 'And you got destroyed. Annihilated. Remember, I heard the songs. You trusted me, you loved me, and I twisted that love into something dark and furious. I twisted you.'

She blanched. 'Yes, you did. I loved you with all my heart, but you couldn't handle that. You pushed me away then and you're pushing me away now. Anytime I get close to you, you panic. You're terrified of letting me love you, aren't you, Luca? That's just about the worst thing you can imagine.'

Hadn't he said as much? She wasn't wrong; he knew that, but he didn't want to admit it, because he knew what the logical progression of that was. He knew the conclusion she might leap to, but it didn't change anything about what he wanted. About what he'd let come of this.

'And why is that? Why are you so damned afraid to just let yourself be loved?'

'You know the answer to that,' he muttered. 'And we're not talking about me right now. This is about Aurora, and how we're going to both be in her life without...'

'No, we're talking about you. Three years ago, I let you push me away because my feelings were hurt, my heart was broken, and it stopped me from seeing that your heart was broken too. It stopped me from seeing *you*. But I see you now—I see you so well, Luca. I see all the parts of you, and guess what?'

He braced. He held himself still. Fear was a throttle at his throat.

'I love you anyway.'

His body reverberated on a tide of terror. Of disgust and anger. And of something else, something that was warm and addictive, something that was urging him to look towards the golden light of what she was saying, rather than into the dark torment of his past.

'I don't want you to love me,' he said, voice harsh, even when he knew the words weren't completely true. He hated himself for being so selfish, but her love…it meant something. It was a validation and a reassurance. It was a balm. But Luca didn't *want* a balm to his pain; he wanted to feel it, deep and hard, for the rest of his life.

'You can control a lot of things in this life, but not who loves you.'

'You'll get over it.'

'Well, it's been three years, and I haven't got over you yet, so why do you think that's going to change any time soon?'

He glared at her, shaking his head. It was preposterous to suggest he'd occupied a place in her heart and mind in these intervening years.

'I'm serious,' she reiterated. 'There hasn't been anyone else for me, Luca. I used to think it was because I've been busy with Aurora, but that's just a lie I told myself to feel better about still loving someone who didn't want me. I had the chance to date. I've been asked out by guys, and Genevieve would always have minded Aurora, but I couldn't bring myself to so much as look at anyone else. Because of you, and what you still meant to me.'

'Stop it,' he said, dragging a hand through his hair. He couldn't hear this. He couldn't hear any of it. Knowing he was the only man to have been with her, the only man who'd worshipped her body, made her cry out with sensual heat—how could that fail to pull at him?

He groaned inwardly, needing to put a stop to this conversation.

'You can't keep fighting me, Luca. I'm here and I want to be here for the rest of our lives. Three years ago, I let you push me away, but that was a profound mistake, and it's not a mistake I intend to make this time around. I can't lose you again, and I don't think you want to lose me.'

'You can't lose something you never had.'

She flinched—as he'd intended. He'd said he didn't want to hurt her, but if that was the only way to get her to accept that he'd never be the Prince Charming she was imagining...

'You're sabotaging your life,' she said softly, surprising him with the strength in her features though, and the fact she was willing to continue this conversation. 'You told me you'd never met anyone like me, that spending a month with me was something you'd never done with another woman. You didn't treat me like some disposable woman you were taking to bed—you treated me like your lifeblood. You treated me like oxygen. *That's* what I should have said to you that morning.'

He closed his eyes on a sinking feeling of fatigue and despair. Imogen had been right; she had changed. Three years ago, he'd been able to control their break-up, even when it had almost destroyed him. Now she was fighting him, tooth and nail. Fighting for them.

'It wouldn't have made any difference.'

'Wouldn't it?'

'No. I needed you out of my life.'

'Because you were scared of what I meant to you.'

His eyes met hers. He should deny it. He knew he should keep shutting down her statements, keep holding to the truth he'd built in his mind. But he was suddenly weary—the kind of weariness that came from carrying a deep, possessive grief for a lifetime. So, he stayed silent, staring at her and beseeching with his eyes for her to understand and relent. To stop pushing him to admit things he couldn't, or didn't want to.

'You were scared of loving me back, even when I think you already did.'

His hands formed fists at his sides; he tried to take strength and command from the physicality of controlling his muscles, to build himself back up cell by cell, but Imogen was pulsing inside of him, weakening him just as he'd always feared she would.

'And you're still scared. You're still running.'

He didn't move to touch his side but instead reached for another wound, mentally. He closed his eyes and remembered the fire. The smell of smoke and burning flesh, the contrast with the cold beneath his feet, the neighbours' strong arms holding him back, the grief and anger and self-recriminations. He reminded himself that he was the worst person in the world, that he'd denied himself her love, and the ability to love her back, because he deserved that, because he owed as much as payment for the crime he'd committed.

'I killed them,' he said quietly, as though that were an answer.

Sympathy washed over Imogen's face.

'You did *not* kill them,' she said, so firmly, with such determination, he almost believed her.

'You weren't there.'

'You were twelve years old and you formed an opinion that you haven't let yourself grow out of. You were not at fault, Luca. You were just a boy—there is nothing more you could have done.'

'The fire—'

'Not your fault. I have no doubt your parents checked it before they went to bed. What happened was an *accident*. A terrible, terrible accident that you will always grieve and regret, but it was not your fault. It's time to stop punishing yourself. It's time to start living.'

'No.' The word was torn from him, so loud that he clamped his jaw and spun away from her, his chest moving with his ragged inhalations. He didn't want to wake Aurora; he didn't want to yell at Imogen either.

'You have to confront this head-on and see how futile your self-loathing is.'

'Why?' He angled his head back in her direction, raking her with his obsidian eyes. 'Why does it matter?'

Her smile was one of torment. 'Because it's not just your life you're ruining, but mine too. Our fates are bound, Luca. They were from the first night we met, from the moment we made love, and they always will be. Not just because of Aurora, but because of us.'

He closed his eyes on a wave of guilt—bigger than he'd ever known. 'I never should have let this happen.'

'I don't think either of us could have stopped it.'

Silence fell, crackling with the pain of the past and the sheer impossibility of any kind of shared future.

'Listen to me.' Imogen's voice emerged husky and raw. 'I believe in my soul that you love me. I don't need to hear you say it to know that it's true. And I think you've been trying to work out a way to have me in your life without betraying this idea you developed as a twelve-year-old that you'd have to spend the rest of your days miserable and alone because of the accident. So you've been putting up electric fences and barriers and holding me at a distance. But then you started to let me in anyway, and you asked me to marry you, and you told me that I am in your blood. I am telling you that this is enough for me.' She tilted her chin with defiance. 'I am saying that I can live my life without you saying that you love me; I can live my life with the understanding that there are parts of you you'll never share with me. I can live my life with those limitations, but I want you in it. I don't want to turn my back on this, or you, again.'

How easy it would have been to take her at face value and accept what she was offering. Wasn't that his dream? To have her without needing to give her more than he wanted to?

But it wouldn't work.

Not because she would make him the happiest man on earth when he'd sworn he would be miserable always, but because the limitations she was willing to accept were an insult to Imogen, and she was worthy of so much better.

'That's not good enough,' he muttered. 'It won't work.'

'Of course it will. It's been working, hasn't it?'

'No. We've been sitting on a ticking time bomb and it's exploding all around us.'

She flinched again.

'I will stay here with you, for the rest of our lives, as your wife, or your lover, or whatever, and I will never tell you I love you again, I will never ask you to love me, if that's what you want.' She sucked in a deep, shudder-

ing breath. 'Or I will leave, in the morning, and that will
be the end of us, once and for all. The decision is yours.'

A muscle throbbed at the base of his jaw as he stared
back at her and felt the tearing of his being. There she
was—the person he wanted, the woman he loved—but
she was across an impossible divide, a barrier he couldn't
straddle.

He had to let her go, but it couldn't be like this. He
couldn't let her doubt what she meant to him; there was no
way he would allow her to go without fully understanding how damned difficult this was for him. He was being
torn apart and she should understand that—if only to save
her from existing in the same hell space he occupied.

'I love you,' he said, so simply, and bizarrely, it didn't
hurt to say the words. It didn't even feel strange, because
loving Imogen was such a part of him now. He didn't
know when that had happened, but she was stitched deep
into his soul and probably always would be. 'But I can't
be with you. I love you, but I refuse to let myself love
you. And if you really love me, you'd understand that, and
you'd accept it.' He closed his eyes on a wave of disgust.
'It's just the way I am, *cara*. It's just who I am.'

CHAPTER THIRTEEN

AT FIRST SHE barely cried. She was in shock. A deep, mind-altering state of confusion and despair, because she was besieged by the kind of grief that made everything unrecognisable. She showered, staring at the tiled wall for so long the lines of the grout began to blur, and then, when she flicked off the water, she sobbed. Her tears fell freely, mingling with the water from the shower, and as she patted her body and face dry, the tears kept falling, silently slipping down her cheeks, as her chest moved with each sob and her body shook on wave after wave of sadness.

Because she'd fought for Luca, and it hadn't been enough.

She'd argued for them. For their relationship, their family, their future—and yes, their love—and he'd pushed her away, just like he had before.

What more could she do?

He'd been so emphatic at first, so clear, so determined, but the more she'd pushed, the more she'd felt his resolve weakening, felt him getting closer and closer to admitting the truth, until he had. And it had been the hardest thing she'd ever have to listen to.

Going into their conversation, she'd had a theory about

how he felt about her, but it had been just that—a theory. A hope. A belief that she couldn't love someone and be so wrong about them.

But when he'd said those words she'd been so desperate to hear, then quickly followed them up with 'but I refuse to let myself love you,' it had broken her heart all over again, and this time, it had broken her heart on his behalf too. She felt so desperate for both of them, for this awful mess they were in. She was still reeling.

She pulled back the cover and curled up in bed, hugging her knees to her chest protectively, squeezing her eyes shut and praying for the relief of sleep; but it didn't come, not for a long, long time. Before it did, Imogen replayed every word, every look, and the tears kept falling.

It was unnaturally silent. So silent he could hear the beating of his heart, its accusatory thumping like a drumbeat of blame. Of recrimination.

He'd told her he didn't want to hurt her again, and that had been true. Regardless, that was exactly what he'd done.

He'd seen it on her face, and he'd never hated himself more.

He cursed the day they'd ever met. For Imogen's sake, he would take it all back, if he could. He would take back every kiss, every touch, every moment that now seemed to shimmer with gold dust because of how special it had been. He would undo it all if it meant he could spare Imogen the pain he'd inflicted upon her again and again.

Darkness wrapped around him, silent and accusatory, and then, somewhere in the small hours of the morning, he heard the worst noise he could possibly imagine: Imogen's sob.

He dropped his head and groaned on a wave of self-disgust.

She must have slept eventually, because Imogen woke just after six, her face pale and eyes puffy. She was not even granted a few scant moments of forgetting—there was no relief in the liminal seconds between sleep and waking, no reprieve from pain. When she woke, it was with the ache of their confrontation at the forefront of her mind, his every word imprinted on her soul.

Acid filled her mouth as she stood and dressed quickly, scraping her hair back into a ponytail before pushing out of her room and moving silently towards Aurora's.

She had to get out of his home. She had to leave.

It was impossible to remain here, feeling as she did, knowing how determined he was to ice her out of his life.

She wanted to silence her brain, to shut down the hateful memories, but if anything, they were growing stronger and louder as she packed Aurora's things. Almost as if the simple act of wrapping up their life here was filling that argument with greater imperative.

Imogen had told Luca that she would fight for him, and she'd done that. She'd fought. She'd been reasonable and calm even when her insides were quivering with sadness and want. He'd rejected her, but not because he didn't want her.

Because he didn't know how to make this work.

Because he was wedded to this idea of guilt, and his answer—the answer of a child, really—was an eye for an eye. He felt he'd taken his parents' and sister's lives, and so his answer was to offer his own in penance.

But what about her life? If he really loved her, surely that counted for something? Surely that could be the beginning of him letting go of this awful pledge of sorrow?

For the briefest moment, hope pierced her heart, like sunshine determinedly finding its way through a thick storm cloud. He loved her. He *loved* her. That had to mean something; she just had to get him to understand that…

After glancing at their still-sleeping daughter, she strode out of Aurora's room in search of Luca, her heart palpitating because if this didn't work, it really would be over. And she desperately didn't want that to be the case.

'What about me?' she asked, when she found him in his study, seated as his desk and staring at the laptop screen. He glanced at her, his expression giving little away.

She noted the glass of Scotch to his left and wondered if he'd poured it because he wanted to take the edge off their conversation.

He lifted a dark brow in silent enquiry, looking to all the world calm and unaffected. But she saw his eyes; she saw through him. She understood him now.

'You're determined to punish yourself for the accident, but what about me?'

His lips compressed as he stared back at her. 'I've told you, I don't want to hurt you.'

'But you are, and you'll keep hurting me, every day that you refuse to let me love you, to let me be loved by you. Are you really okay with that?'

He reached for the Scotch and curled his hands around the glass, gripping it without drinking. 'I've told you—'

'You've told me nothing,' she said with a slash of her hand through the air. 'Nothing that makes sense, anyway.'

'You know why I am this way.'

'You know what you haven't told me, Luca? You know what you never say?'

He was silent.

'What would your parents want?'

He stood up as though she'd electrocuted him, Scotch still clutched in one hand. 'Don't.'

'You speak of them with love. Admiration. You describe a childhood that was happy and filled with the certainty that you were adored. Would they have wanted you to be alone and miserable for the rest of your life?'

'It's not about what they would have wanted, it's what I deserve.'

She expelled an angry breath. 'I don't believe that. I don't believe that for even a second, but even if I did— what about me? What about what I deserve? Can't you just try, try a little, to put this aside for my sake?'

He closed his eyes, so she had no way of knowing if she was getting through to him, no way of knowing if he was starting to understand how his path of self-loathing was affecting her.

'I'm letting you go because of what you deserve. I recognise that you should have so much more than this.'

'I don't want more than this; I just want you.'

He shook his head. 'It's impossible.'

'No, it's not. You could fight for this. You could fight for me, for us.'

He stared at her, as though her words were torture, but also, vitally, he was listening.

'For your aunt and uncle,' she continued, hope stretching in her heart. 'Your cousins. For Aurora. You've built an enormous fortress, and a crocodile-infested moat around yourself, and yet here we all are: people who love you, who will *always* love you, no matter how hard you push us away. Maybe *that's* what you deserve? To know that there is nothing that you can do that would make us stop loving you?'

'Don't,' he groaned. 'I don't want to hear it.'

'But you need to hear it, you need to feel it.' She closed the distance between them and caught his hand, pressed it to her chest. 'You have my heart, Luca. You hold it in your hands, as much now as you did three years ago. Please, I'm begging you—don't throw this away as though it means nothing.'

'It means *everything*. I told you that. This isn't a question of love. It's not about whether or not I love you, or believe you love me.' His voice was thick with emotion. 'I am choosing a different path, something other than this—'

'I can't let you do that,' she whispered. 'I just can't.'

'It's not your decision.'

He needed her to understand that. Damn it, why wouldn't she hear him?

He'd never seen Imogen like this. She was acting as though her whole life depended on his acceptance of her argument—didn't she understand? He couldn't give her that!

Only Imogen reached up and grabbed his jaw with her fingers, holding his face steady so their eyes had to meet and stick, and something inside of him shifted and gave way, something important and vital. Something he'd always relied on, to hold people at bay. His whole world seemed to be shifting—in fact, tipping off its axis—so nothing was recognisable now.

'Listen to me, Luca Romano.' He *was* listening. Intently. 'I love you. I love you because you are good and decent.' Her eyes bore into his, long and hard. 'You are good, and you deserve to be happy.' His first instinct was to fight that—or rather, it would have been. But now, her words washed over him, and he actually let them. Not just wash over him, but seep in, deep into his soul. 'Let me spend the rest of our lives enjoying that happiness with you. Just let me love you—and when you're ready, love me back.' Her voice was husky, and yet somehow reassuring. 'It's that simple.'

He shook his head, but not hard enough to dislodge her grip. She stood up onto the tips of her toes and brushed her lips over his. His heart jolted. 'I love you,' she repeated, and the words continued to seep into him. 'And you are worthy of that love.'

His breath shuddered and it was another release, of the old hatreds and blame, the guilt, the determination to destroy his life because of the past.

'I love you,' she said again, like an incantation. 'I'm not going anywhere. I can't.'

He closed his eyes in a wave of relief. Imogen leaving was the last thing he wanted; he'd grappled with that all night and now knew it to be true. He wanted her to stay. He *needed* her.

She was his family.

He lifted a hand to her cheek, touching her as if to reassure himself that she was real. 'I don't know what to say,' he admitted, then shook his head, because that was only part of it. He placed his Scotch glass down on his desk, then put one hand behind her back, drawing her to him. 'Even if you stay, I can't promise this will be easy. I don't want to hurt you, it's just… I don't know how to do this…any of it. I'm…lost.'

* * *

The honesty of that admission pulled at Imogen's heart-strings as nothing else could. Here was big, tough, lone wolf Luca Romano, the man who could do *anything*, admitting that this was new to him. She leaned forward and pressed a kiss to his chest.

'I know that. I get it. I'm not expecting you to change overnight. You've spent decades hating yourself, blaming yourself for that awful accident, and walling yourself away from anyone who got close to you. I know there are some instincts you're going to have to work to unlearn. But I love you, I'm not going anywhere…and I have faith in you. I know you can do this; I know you can let me in, Luca.'

He dropped his forehead to hers, inhaling deeply. 'I can't let you again,' he admitted on a groan. 'But *Cristo*, nor can I live with hurting you, with messing this up…'

'So don't mess it up,' she said with a lift of one shoulder. 'You're a really smart guy. You've got this.'

He furrowed his brow as if trying to make sense of the world he was stepping into, of the world she was showing him.

'Are you saying…you really want to marry me?'

Imogen laughed softly. 'I'm saying I love you, but no. I'm not going to marry you. Not yet.'

His frown deepened.

'Let's walk before we can run. I love you, and you love me, so let's wait and get married down the track, when we're used to this situation, when you've met my parents and I've met your aunt and uncle, when you're able to love me without feeling as though it's some kind of a betrayal,' she added gently. 'Let's wait and do it all slowly, let's do it properly.'

'Yes,' he exhaled with a breath of relief. 'I want that for you.'

'Oh, Luca. I want it for both of us.'

Genevieve was, in the end, not such an enormous stumbling block. Whether it was seeing the pair of them together, or Luca's determination to win her over, it didn't take long before Genevieve was disavowing any possible reason to hate Luca and instead singing his praises. He was 'such a good dad' and 'wonderfully supportive of Imogen,' and when Luca and Imogen drove out to the Cotswolds to meet Imogen's parents, Genevieve went with them.

She continued to help with Aurora, having the little girl some weekends so Luca and Imogen could escape for quick romantic trips. They always felt that they were making up for lost time, and Genevieve seemed to understand that.

Reuniting with Luca's aunt and uncle was an emotional and heart-wrenching experience—but also one of joy. They were overwhelmed with love for Aurora, and when Imogen finally saw pictures of baby Angelica, she could see for herself that the two girls were indeed like twins. Luca's aunt and uncle doted on Aurora, and they couldn't stop staring at Luca, at how much he'd changed, at how grown-up he was, how successful. They'd kept a folder of newspaper clippings, showing his various successes; their pride was so obvious.

They loved him. They understood why he'd pushed them away, but they'd missed him, and they were eternally grateful to Imogen for helping him find his way back to them.

And so it was, on one such trip back to see Luca's family, when they returned to his villa in Tuscany for the night, and lay on a blanket beneath the stars and among the vines, Imogen was reflecting on how glad she was to have fought for this, on how much had been at stake, and Luca's thoughts were apparently of a similar bent. He lifted up onto one elbow and smiled across at her, a smile that radiated true happiness and inner peace, and reached for her hand, intertwining their fingers.

'I love you.'

Three little words that meant so much, and all the more because she knew Luca had never intended to say them to another soul.

'And I've been thinking about something.'

Her eyes scanned his face. 'Oh?'

'What I said to you that morning—that you would be easy to replace.'

'Luca, it doesn't matter.'

But his lips quirked downwards. 'You brought it up, the first time we came here.' He nodded towards the villa. 'You said those words had tortured you for a long time.'

'It all seems like so long ago.' She furrowed her brow. 'It feels like something that happened to someone else, not us.'

'I agree. But I need to tell you something I didn't dare admit back then.'

She held her breath, no idea what would come next, yet somehow secure enough in their love to know the bubble wouldn't burst.

'I didn't replace you. I couldn't.' He brushed a thumb over her lips, staring at her as if mesmerised.

'I don't understand.'

'I met women. I thought about asking them home with me. Something always held me back. At the time, I told myself it was further punishment of my sins—not just towards my parents and sister but also towards you. I told myself I didn't deserve even the pleasure of sex any more. But really, I just didn't want to be with anyone but you.'

Imogen's jaw dropped. 'You're saying there was no one else after me?'

'I'm saying that, yes.'

She shook her head a little, and tears flooded her eyes. 'Oh, Luca.' She bit into her lip. 'You have no idea how much it hurt, to imagine you with other women.'

'Actually, I have a fair idea. You are not the only one who played out those scenarios. I was a glutton for punishment, quite literally, and the knowledge that you had undoubtedly moved on was a frequent source of self-flagellation for me.'

She closed her eyes on a wave of pity and sadness. 'We wasted so much time.'

'I didn't admit to myself that I loved you, but I knew you were irreplaceable, that it would be impossible to even try.'

She wriggled forward so their bodies connected. 'I'm glad you came to your senses finally.'

His lips quirked. 'You and me both.'

'When you came to the bar that night, was it because you were looking for me?'

He scanned her face thoughtfully. 'Undoubtedly. There was so much I didn't admit to myself—so much I didn't understand. But the second I heard your voice and then turned around and saw you, it was like the stars were aligning for me. I felt a burst of life and adrenaline, a need that rocked me to my core. I just needed you,' he said with a lift of his shoulder. 'I'll always need you.'

'And I'll always be here.' She kissed him beneath the blanket of stars, knowing that truer words had never been spoken.

* * *

The next morning, she received the email from the record label executive; they wanted to meet the following week. It was an email that began a juggernaut—of meetings and recordings and, eventually, a career that would defy all of Imogen's wildest dreams. A career that Luca was immensely proud of her for, as he watched from the sidelines with love and admiration for the woman he loved and the talent she possessed.

After she'd recorded her first studio album, and before things became too wild and fast-paced, Luca arranged a night out with Imogen—to celebrate her success. Only it was a night like no other. With Genevieve ensconced at their home on Aurora duty, Imogen and Luca were conveyed to the closest airport and his private jet, which traversed the short distance to Paris, touching down in the late afternoon. They were whisked to the Eiffel Tower, and straight to the top of it, where they stood and sipped champagne as the sun went down and the sky filled with gold and mauve and everything was glorious. Imogen was utterly transfixed by the view, so she didn't notice at first that Luca had crouched to the ground, until she spun around to point something out to him and found him on one knee.

'Luca.' She lifted a hand to her mouth, fingers trembling.

'*Cara mia*, you know how I feel about you. You know how much I love and adore you, how much I worship you. I am indebted to you for bringing me back to life, out of the fog of a grief I thought I would never escape. You are responsible for every single piece of happiness I will ever feel in my life. You have already given me one of the greatest gifts with our beautiful Aurora, yet here

I am, asking you for another gift. Would you do me the honour of being my wife?'

Imogen had forestalled the idea of marriage in the past, because she had known the most important part of their journey—at that point in time—revolved around Luca's recovery. Luca accepting that he was worthy of love, of happiness, of a future untinged by the grief of his past. He had recovered, though. Not fully, but day by day, step by step, smile by smile, he was finally moving on, and she no longer believed his past had any ability to hurt them.

She curved her hand around his cheek, smiling and nodding, tears in her eyes. 'Yes,' she said, her voice high in pitch. 'Of course I'll marry you.'

Her eyes dropped then to the ring box he held, and the stunning, enormous solitaire diamond at its centre. He removed it and slid it onto her finger, and at that exact moment, the sun gave a last fiery burst before dipping behind the buildings on the horizon, casting rays of gold from her finger—a metaphor for their future if ever she'd seen one.

They didn't wait to marry. Six weeks was more than enough time to plan a simple ceremony saturated in love and affection. They chose his villa as the location, and Luca's assistant organised every last detail perfectly. There were marquees in case it rained, bohemian rugs on the ground so guests could take off their shoes and relax, exquisite food, prosecco in abundance, and a wonderful local band played music late into the night. They even played the song Imogen had written, that had been such a global success, and Luca sang along to it, grinning at Imogen, because those words were a part of the fabric of their past. They were a lesson, for both of them, about feelings, and love, and not wasting opportunities.

They would never waste their second chance; it was a pledge they'd made in their wedding vows, and intended to make to one another always.

When news broke that Imogen's first single had hit number one on the charts in several countries around the world, including the UK and America, one might have thought it was the most exciting news she'd received that day. And it was certainly wonderful, but nothing compared to the two bright lines that stared back at her from a little white pregnancy test.

It hadn't been planned, and yet they hadn't exactly been careful. There'd been slip-ups from time to time, when passion had moved them. Their honeymoon in Egypt had been so romantic, and when Imogen counted back the dates on her calendar, she suspected it had indeed been the night after their wedding that had placed new life inside of her.

She pressed a hand to her stomach, her heart fluttering in her chest, because the suspicion that had been growing for the last few weeks had finally been confirmed.

Only, they had a house full of people! Imogen's parents and sister had come to celebrate her success, as well as some friends from the bar, and Brock, the executive who'd discovered her. The house was full and brimming with excitement, Imogen's album playing in the background as they all talked excitedly about what the number one news might mean for her. 'Magazine covers, definitely.' Genevieve grinned, and Imogen's head swirled.

'Are you okay?' Luca caught her in the kitchen, making a cup of tea. 'You seem distracted.'

'Oh, I—guess I am.'

'It's overwhelming?' he said, lifting her chin.

She bit into her lip. 'It is, it is. It's just... I've hardly been able to think about the album, to be honest.'

His brows drew together. 'Really? Something more exciting on your mind?'

He'd said it as a joke, teasing her, but Imogen nodded, then quickly scanned the room to make sure they were still alone. She lifted up onto her tiptoes and whispered the news in his ear, then pulled back to see his reaction.

It was impossible to interpret all the feelings that flitted across his face, but her heart lifted to see him smile. 'For real?'

She nodded. 'You're happy?'

'Happy? I'm ecstatic. Oh, Imogen, it's the best news I've ever heard. Aurora is the meaning of our lives, I know that, but there is so much I missed. So much I didn't get to support you through. I want to be there with you this time, through the pregnancy, the birth, the early days. I want to see Aurora become a big sister, to watch her beam with pride when she holds her little brother or sister. I'm beyond happy. Thank you.'

'I didn't do anything.'

'Oh, yes, you did. You brought me back to life—you stood by me and made me wake up, and now I am living some kind of fantasy. You are everything to me, my darling.'

She kissed him, her heart soaring, her happiness impossible to contain.

They were blessed with three more children, and Imogen had more than ten number one singles during her career. She became famous the world over, but none of that mattered to her. It was a by-product of doing what she loved, that was all. The people that really mattered to her were the people she'd loved and been loved by before her success; she never lost her grounding. From time to time, she went back to the bar that held such a special place in her heart, to sing for unsuspecting crowds. It always garnered an enormous response, and each time, as the night wore on, and social media lit up with the knowledge she was there, the place would get packed, but Imogen barely noticed. When she played at that place, it was like stepping back in time, and memories of her and Luca, meeting in the bar, beginning their story together there, were what she felt most of all.

When the bar went on the market, they bought it in an instant, and Imogen put her energy into turning it into a place for fledgling musicians to come and perform. She saw it as her duty to support those attempting to break into the industry, and her connections ensured record label executives and social media music influencers were always in attendance.

Ten years after their wedding, in a sign that the past was still very much a part of them, even when it could no longer hurt them, Luca and Imogen stood side by side as they opened a burns unit at a top hospital, in his family's name. With state-of-the-art technology and some of the best specialists in the world, the unit would become a beacon to those who needed it. His parents were gone, but never forgotten; his sister was someone they spoke of often. Indeed, a family photograph of Luca, his parents and sister now had pride of place in their home, and Imogen smiled at them whenever she walked by. She hoped that somehow they knew just how happy Luca was, how well he was doing, and that he'd found his way to a family that truly loved him, and always would.

* * * * *